Tawnie and Enrique` (Henry)

Her Master, His Slave

A Novel by Toni Mariani

COPYRIGHT PAGE

This work is self published by Author Toni Mariani, and assisted by Amazon tools for self publishing.

Her Master, His Slave. 2017 Toni Mariani

ISBN- 10:1544676190

ISBN-13:9781544676197

DEDICATION

THIS WORK IS DEDICATED TO THOSE WHO ARE BEHIND ME, SLEEPING IN DEATH. ONE DAY THEY WILL HEAR THE CALL TO AWAKEN FROM SLEEP AND RISE. ON THAT DAY WE WILL WELCOME THEM TO PARADISE HERE ON EARTH. THAT INCLUDES MY FAMILY LINE ALL THE WAY BACK TO THE BEGINNING. SO MANY PEOPLE TO MENTION BUT I WILL THANK MY MOTHER WHO AS A YOUNG GIRL HERSELF BROUGHT ME INTO THE WORLD, AND THOUGH I WAS SICK AND NEAR DEATH, SHE KEPT ME NOURISHED AS WELL AS SHE COULD.

Contact Information

brigittenrich@aol.com

bware@shebogan.k12.wi.us

https://www.amazon.com/author/tonimariani

https://www.facebook.com/earthtotoni

https://www.facebook.com/Author-Toni-Mariani

TABLE OF CONTENTS

Acknowledgments

Table of contents

ACKNOWLEDGMENTS

I'd like to acknowledge the cover image artist Jimmy and his assistant Andrea. Jimmy is widely known as a long-time model and design artist. I love music and will always put my favorite songs in my work. This work includes songs by Mtume, Freddie Jackson, Zapp & Roger, Betty Wright, Main Ingredient, Tina Marie & Rick James, Marvin Gaye, Luther Ingram, Skylark, Roberta Flack, Keith Washington.

I also want to acknowledge Olivia Gaines for introducing me to Jimmy. Thanks lady.

Wikipedia.org provided the information on Lieutenant-General John Clifford Pemberton who was in fact on the road, on the date mentioned in the story. He was a Northerner who traded in his US allegiance to serve in the Confederate Army, turning his back on his two brothers who fought for the Union.

1 CHAPTER

"Mama, thank you so much for the goodbye party, and I want you to know I will call you at least once a month and Bry and I will bring the children back twice a year, at least. We want you all to watch them grow up and daddy wants to teach the boys how to fish. Give me one more hug and please stop crying, you're going to make me cry and my mascara's gonna run."

"Tawnie, your daddy and I are going to miss you so much, I hope you know. We can't wait to come down, visit you all and see the property. From the pictures it still looks grand, and we are so happy that the agent accepted your offer. Did he say why you two were able to get it at such a steal?" Mrs. Hazelton asked her daughter and son-in-law as she hugged them.

"Just that, because of family ties he couldn't see trying to ask more for it. He said the names of all the families are written down in an old ledger and your names were written there too. Well the name Hazelton was there so we were able to put a small deposit and earnest money down and got the mortgage without any trouble. I plan on teaching music and Tawnie will continue with her appearances on occasion, but mainly recording theme music for movies," Bryen tried to reassure the Hazelton's. He knew that Rollins, Diedra and their five daughters were close and everyone hated to lose another loved one to a move. The oldest daughter was out in California working on films as an assistant director. Aubree was working hard and loving her career choice and did not make it home nearly enough to satisfy her parents. He would make sure that Tawnie did better.

"As long as you keep your promise to call on schedule and visit, and let us know when we can come down, we will be satisfied. Is everything packed up?" Rollins Hazelton asked.

"Yes daddy. We only have a few things with us, a few personal items. Everything else is being driven down by the company hired by Bry's employer, MSU."

"It won't be bad. We're going to stop and do a bit of site-seeing passing through Tennessee. I want to see the Smokies and Tawnie wants to see a few of the old plantations to see how they're being restored to their former glory," Bryen told his father-in-law who stood looking skeptical.

Rollins would miss his second oldest daughter, the favorite daughter because she was the sensitive one, the one who loved too strongly, even those who were almost too sick to love. Rollins was a big man, standing six-feet-four-inches, but when it came to how tall he felt this moment having to tell his beautiful tender-hearted daughter good-bye for who knew how long, he felt small indeed. Rollins was a manager at the county meat processing house and was a favorite among his colleagues and employees. He was a singer and during his two tours of duty in the Army, had a singing group that performed in clubs wherever they were sent around the world. His wife Diedra, mother of his five daughters and Tawnie's sisters was involved in helping teachers apply for special grants for their classrooms. There was never enough money for the states to spread around, so extra funding was sought each year from the federal Department of Education to off-set classroom costs. Diedra would find out what resources would be available for the next school year and go after them with a vengeance, knowing that every little bit helped. She was a college educated woman who trained as a teacher but when her children came along, they had to decide which came first; her career or family. As a couple it was decided that the best contribution they could make would be to send out responsible, compassionate, well-educated daughters into the world and the best way to ensure that happened, would be to take charge of raising them herself

7

as a full-time, stay at home parent. The tools she used in schools were also valued in her home, and she pinched every penny she could to make sure her girls had whatever they needed, plus a few extra wants.

Diedra was a five-feet-nine-inch beauty herself, and had a lot of competition in her day for Rollins Hazelton. They met in junior high and he went after her then, but her parents would not allow her to date, so he waited until their senior year in high school to ask her out. Several years later after steady dating, after Diedra ran a few of Rollins' 'side pieces' away with some choice words, and her return from college they were married. Rollins wore his Army uniform dress colors and looked like a movie star. They each were filled with pride for the way the other one looked and right-a-way settled down to family life.

After kissing the three little ones, Rollins held Diedra while she waved and threw air kisses to the family as they headed down the road to their new life in Mississippi.

∞∞∞

"Bry, who knew daddy would be so pragmatic about this move? I thought it would be mama sending us off with assurances, but she flipped the script on me and wanted the most reassurance."

"That's the way it happens sometimes. You saw the way it was with my mom and dad, the opposite of yours. But with promises to call and visit like you made, they calmed down. You have the keys to the new house and all the information we need to get a hold of the utility companies right?"

"Yep, in fact I called and asked them to turn on all the services in two days. I figured that would give us time to explore the states we travel through and other plantation homes we pass the further south we get. Are my babies excited about traveling to a new place?" Tawnie asked her three beautiful children in the back seat.

"Yes mama!" she heard chorused back to her.

"Let daddy and I know when you need the bathroom, okay?"

"Yes mama!" she heard again. While she listened to the radio play her favorite tunes, such as the one on now by Marvin Gaye, Sexual Healing, she thought over the last few years and each of her three births. As a mother she couldn't be more proud of her three little ones. With their father's genes from his Italian roots, her multicultural background including Scandinavians, what the genetic makeup in these three produced was truly astounding. She thought her father-in-laws children with his two women were gorgeous, but her three were even more so. Maybe she was a little prejudiced, but she didn't think so. She scooted over closer to her husband, her man, her lover and her life Bryen. As she ran her hands through his thick wavy black mane, she thought over their life together and how they met all those years ago. She thought over the tragedy in college that resulted in the death of Bryen's brother Rico but she didn't want to dwell on that so she turned the next song up and looked back at her babies, who were now dozing. Luther Ingram's If Loving You Is Wrong, made for a more pleasant thought train. Thoughts of Rico often crept in her consciousness, sometimes persecuting her with self-recriminations that maybe it was her fault or maybe she could have done more to help him seek treatment. In reality, there was nothing she could have done, because the mentally ill need treatment that they are mostly in denial of, will self-medicate to ignore it and keep others from finding out how truly ill they really are. That was the case with her brother-in-law, but she wasn't going to think about Rico right now. She moved even closer to her husband and rubbed his thigh.

"Tawnie, now you know you can't do things like this when I'm driving. Do you want to get down the road to the next state tonight, or get a hotel so I can drive my cock in you? Whichever you want I can give you, sweetheart. You know I'm always ready to make love to you. It's probably time to get pregnant again anyway. Is that what you want?" Bryen asked his beautiful hazel eyed, honey-colored love of his life.

"Babe, of course I'm always ready to serve you up some good lovin, but I do want to get down the road some before dark. I hate trying to figure the roads out in the dark, and I don't want you overtired, so for now keep going. And about getting pregnant, I would appreciate waiting a year so we both can get established in Grenada."

"I think that's a great plan, even though I love seeing you pregnant, and of course getting there is the most fun of all. How ya doing baby?"

"I'm good, no worries. You okay?"

"Yep, but I can stand a smooch right here," Bryen said pointing at his cheek. Tawnie leaned in and gave him one where he pointed. She wasn't about to bring up her reoccurring thoughts about Rico. She wanted to squash her troubled imaginings not cause Bryen to start having those of his own. "Why don't you lean back and nap while I get us down the road. Then we can eat lunch in the car, keep going; about six this evening we can stop, get a motel, get dinner and rest for the night."

"Sounds good baby, but let me know if you get tired."

2 CHAPTER

Two and a half days later Bryen pulled up to their new home. It was a humid sticky evening and the family arrived around dusk, but the sounds of the south were music to Tawnie's ears. She loved music and all around her she could hear a harmonious melody of sounds. She heard birds tweeting to each other, probably saying their goodnights, a barred owl, the scratching sounds of possible bats, a coyote or fox, a wild cat or bobcat and of courses thousands of crickets all coming together to awaken the night. Though it was really too late to look around, they decided to take a quick peek before it got pitch black out. Bryen led the family down a paving stone covered path around the side of the house and on toward the back lawn. Tawnie looked up and saw what was making the scratching bat sounds, an actual colony of them, swooping together in their nightly dance to catch their meal for the next twenty-four hours. She hoped they stayed aloft and didn't swoop near the children. Bryen stopped and they looked around the back which stretched far out toward a body of water. It was too dark to see if it was a creek or larger, but they decided to wait until morning to explore further. Whatever it was should be on the map they received from the realtor, with regards to the property boundary. Bryen hoped it would be large enough to catch some catfish.

"Well, we made it safely thank God. Let's go on in and get washed off and we can do the rest tomorrow," he said while yawning. "I bet you three are sleepy, cause daddy is. Mama, are you sleepy?" he asked Tawnie winking. He wanted to make sure she knew he would be wanting to make love to her to initiate the new house.

"I sure am daddy," she said stretching. "Okay my babies, lets run upstairs and wash our faces and hands and get in our jammies." She leaned into Bryen and kissed his luscious lips. "I'll meet you in the master tub, if you run grab the few things from the car. I bet I'll beat you?"

"Uh unh!" he teased her. "If you do, your choice of positions."

"Oh goody, because I'm probably too tired for what you had in mind for your choice," she laughed and kissed him again.

"Back in a minute," he said as he swatted her butt.

As she and her children ascended the stairs where all bedrooms were, he watched her go. He was so in love with her he thought. Just as much as when they first met in fifth grade. But they were grown now, and he wanted to make love to his lovely wife. As he hurried back to the car he listened to night calls between coyotes, thinking about the next day. He was hired to teach music and was looking for a full professorship. He assumed he'd eventually get moved up because the staff were older and some were looking forward to retiring. With Tawnie working from home, he knew she would need a couple extra hands to assist her so he better start thinking of asking around for a grandmotherly type who could lend a pair of loving hands for his babies. Not so much babies any more he thought, remembering his oldest son Miguel was nearly six now. Well technically his brother Rico's sperm gave him life but he was the nurturer, the true father. Bryen thought over the decision he and Tawnie had made to never share with Miguel the true nature of his parentage, the fact that his father raped his mother while she was unconscious and full of a date rape drug he had given her. What child would ever need to know that about their parent, including the fact that his father was then shot down like a mad dog when trying to escape from the FBI. No, he would protect his children from that knowledge at all cost. Having a shared genetic makeup, there should never be a need for anyone to know. Now to hurry back to his wife.

After Tawnie got the kids wiped down and tucked in, she set up the turn table and put on an album of Smokey Robinson and the Miracles that she loved more than his new stuff. She ran herself and Bryen a hot bubble bath, pouring her signature scent in the water, orange blossom and vanilla bean. It was a natural herbal mix created by an herbalist just for her. Supposedly it was a remedy for aches and pains all wrapped up in a beauteous scent. She was vain enough to still want her man to want to take a bite out her neck during foreplay. For some reason this drove him wild. Maybe the creators got it wrong and it was really an aphrodisiac instead of medicinal, she thought and chuckled out loud.

"What are you giggling at sweet thang?" Bryen came in the bathroom at that moment. Since she was still bent over the tub nude, he swatted her plump juicy rear end, cradling it and bending over kissing it. "Umm, yummy, mine all mine," he said while hurriedly undressing. "Kids all tucked in?" he asked Tawnie.

"They were practically snoring before their little heads hit the pillows. I think the humidity and the night sounds will make it nice for sleeping. Once we get done here I will be just as dead on my feet I'm sure. What about you? You're not going in tomorrow, right?"

"No. I won't go in until next Monday. I took a few days to make sure the movers put everything in its place from the basement to the attic, and I have to be around when they come back with the inventory list. I also want to go down to the staffing agency and see if there is a grandmotherly type looking to sit with children for a few hours a day. If you want to you can sit in while I interview a few ladies, just to make sure she would meld with our family. Of course I know your taste but it's only fair that you have a choice in choosing someone you'll be leaving your precious babies in the care of for a few hours. And baby, make sure you hang your schedule in the office so I know what to expect from one day to the next."

"Of course, Bry. This place is huge, do you think we should get a live in couple who can help with the lawn care, garden and pond cleaning? I think we should also think about a in-ground swimming pool like you guys had back home. I liked that Frank and the ladies had everything right there at home for all their children to play, share and love, at home first. I think I'd like the couple to be middle-aged, the woman can clean and be available to do laundry. Maybe she can help out with cooking when we plan to have guest in from the University or for my book club teas I plan on starting."

"Oh yeah? When did you think up teas?" Bryen asked sounding skeptical.

"I've had the idea for awhile now. There are so many talented writers out there who could probably use a little attention, so I want to post a card requesting art lovers to think about joining us for book discussions twice a month. I'll write something up and if you'd hang it in the hall near your room I'd appreciate it."

"Of course, baby. Now bring your bad self closer to this Anaconda over here waiting to sink into your secret garden," Bryen answered in his deep sultry voice.

"That's funny Bry. Where did you hear that expression, secret garden?" Tawnie snickered.

"It's a new cut out by Quincy Jones and a few male artists. I'll get it in a few days so you can hear it. Barry White, Al B. Sure, James Ingram and El Debarge all have a share in it. You smell delicious woman; so good I just want to take a bite out of you. But instead I will touch you here, and here, and can I touch you right there? How does that feel?" he asked Tawnie while stroking her clit to encourage it to come out and play. It was obvious that she loved it since she had to force herself to remain still and not writhe beneath his hand. "I love your skin; the touch, the smell, the way it glistens when water touches it. I love your lips, the way they both smile and open for me when I do this. I love your walk, your curves, everything about you but especially the way you move under me when I touch you there. Baby, I love everything about you; I've always loved you," Bryen admitted as he held Tawnie as she screamed out her orgasm. "Yes my angel, I love it when you scream from my touches, when I make you cum. What's my name?"

"Bry, oh Bry aiuto, ahhh, ooohhh, it feels soooo good!" Tawnie cried out while stretching her arms over her head, stiffening up with her second orgasm. "Now, pronto a sgommare, turn around and ride me baby," Bryen purred in her ear. He lifted and turned her to face him, positioning his cock in one hand while she opened herself up for him and eased her tight passage around his bobbing bulging rod. "That's good, fammi entrare, Tawnie, ride daddy's big snake. Oh, precious, I love you so. Ah, it's so good. Il serpentone si sta preparando a lasciarsi andare Tawnie. Are you ready, come with me, aaahhhh! Hmmmm!" he called out as he reached the precipice, shot his load and tumbled back down slowly while Tawnie squeezed him dry. They sat locked together as each caught their breathe. Tawnie stroked his back and ran her hands through his long shoulder length dark locks, purring words of love.

"I love you so much Bry. Now I know I can sleep through the night. Can you help me up, then walk with me to kiss the babies one last time."

"Of course sweetheart. It's been a long day," he said as he lifted her under her arms and out of the tub, then joined her as he eased a fluffy bath sheet around them both.

3 CHAPTER

Over the next few days Bryen and Tawnie settled in to their historical home, on what was left of a twelve-hundred acre plantation. After years of selling parcels off to relatives, the ten acres was nothing compared to in its heyday. They interviewed five grandmotherly type widows and three couples and offered the positions to Magdalena, called Maggs who would assist as nanny; Jedediah and Rose, a couple who moved into the apartment in the basement. Jed would take care of the outside, including the body of water and pool after it was built, and Rose would clean, do laundry for everyone and special occasion cooking.

Bryen set up Tawnie's home office and music room so she could teach music and write orchestral arrangements that would be sold for movies and theatrical stage plays. On the Sunday before Bryen went back to work teaching music at the University and acting as band leader, the family was out in the vegetable garden trying to decide what they would plant and where. Music was playing on a turn table set up outside the back shed that held the tools and was near the gardens. Jed was trimming bushes and giving special attention to lovely magnolia trees, while the babies ran around free and wild. Tawnie asked Bryen, "Bry, I'd like to plant lily of the valley about here but they are considered to be poisonous. They have a wonderful sweet smell , a beautiful bell -like flower and could be used to keep away certain bugs. The trouble is the babies are so small and might pick one, eat it and get sick. What do you think? Do you think they'd understand if we explain they are not to touch it?"

"I think so. Repetition is the key to enforcement and with Maggs watching them closely along with us, we can go ahead and try. Miguel, you are our big boy and you can help us with the two little ones can't you?" Bryen called out to his oldest. The two toddlers, Diego three years and Aribella two years, and was called Ari were using plastic shovels to dig their own little gardens.

"Yes I can pops. I don't go to school this year so I can help," Miguel said looking between Tawnie and Bryen nodding his head. Because he wasn't quite six the principal suggested that he wait another year before starting kindergarten. Tawnie was secretly happy because she wasn't ready to let him out into the big world any way. One reason she worked from home was to have her babies around her and be the major contributor to the knowledge they gained, so that knowledge could be turned into wisdom that would prepare them to lead useful lives.

"I think a grouping of calla lilies could stand there in the center of the arrangement, giving it the height it needs for symmetry. The edges could be filled with baby's breath, and behind it I'd fill the beds with hostas, which would have enough shading from the height of the lilies. Jed is there a gardening center where all these things can be obtained and brought in easily?" she asked the new gardener.

"Oh, yes ma'am, real easy. The owners use to deliver to this place frequently years ago. When the last of the family died off, there was no one left to give orders," Jed shared.

Tawnie listened to Jed with half an ear because she was looking around entranced by her surroundings. She took deep lung full's of garden air, inhaling the earthy smells of spring, letting it all move through her. She closed her eyes, listened to the rustle of wings that each bird made as they fluttered here and there, and then bent down to take her shoes off so her feet could feel dirt. The earth was heating up with the increased hours of sunlight, and nature was waking up to devour her bounty. Tawnie heard calls of the sparrows, doves and even pigeons. They each had their own voices, their own songs shared between two alone, and she heard distinct differences of each. Some rustled through trees and others stayed closer to the ground, pecking for grubs and worms to feed their mates. Spring was her favorite time of year with autumn a close second. Life was being renewed and this was the mating season, a time when creatures everywhere were seeking for one like them to join and produce the next generation. It thrilled her to know that soon she too would open herself up to receive Bryen's life giving sperm and have another child with him. Not yet though. There was still much to do.

"I'll jot a sketch of the plantings we discussed and pin it to the bulletin board Jed. Let me know when you're ready and I'll come help. I don't want you to have all the fun with this project because I love digging in the earth too," she laughed.

"I know that's right! I'm glad we'll work together. Are you a water lover too? You know that pond is deep and is filled with all manner of fish and other water creatures."

Bryen spoke up with, "We heard the sounds coming from there all night. It makes for good loving music."

"Bry, Jed does not need to hear all that!" she scolded him with laughter in her voice.

"Jed is married, so I'm sure he knows exactly what I'm talking about, huh Jed?"

"Oh, yes sir I do. Rose and I birthed six children of our own. They are spread out all around the country but we get to see them occasionally when home calls to them. When the full moon is shining bright you can hear the calls of the night especially loud. I have tape recordings of it that I made for a professor at the University."

"Ooooh! I would love to do that. Great idea Jed. I could use it to put it in a piece of music I'm putting together for a movie producer. He has a movie that's about completed called *Down by the Bayou*."

"Are you close to being done with that one Tawnie?" Bryen wanted to know.

"Just about. With the natural accompaniments added it will be a masterpiece!" she told him.

"Mama, daddy, come see what we found!" Diego called to his parents.

"Okay baby. Jed, we'll talk more soon. Let me know if you need anything," Bryen told Jed while moving toward his young ones. He wondered what the three found. He took Tawnie's hand and they followed the sounds of giggling from Ari, who was big for her age. She ran around behind her brothers like a little tomboy. When they reached the children, they looked where they stood pointing and saw a little shack. "Well, what have we hear?" he asked using his spooky voice to give the kids a thrill.

"Daddy, stop you scare me with that voice," Ari said laughing. He knew that the opposite was true. She was the one who he could tickle the most, and when playing hide and seek she was never found but lasted the longest until either he or Tawnie called quits. "Come inside mama. This is my play house. Diego, Miguel and mine. We live here now and want you to fix it!" she ordered her parents.

"Oh, this is nice. Can daddy and mama come in and see your play house Ari?" Tawnie asked her baby girl.

"Yes mama, but you have to bring a broom, chair, curtain . . .what else Diego?"

"Food!" Diego yelled.

"Yes, but we gonna garden and grow food too," Ari told her parents helpfully.

"That will be a big help because your brothers like to eat, huh Miguel?" Bryen asked the oldest.

"Yep. But we're growing boys, right Diego?"

"Yep!" Diego shouted laughing.

"Well, it looks like with a little paint, a mop bucket along with Ari's broom and chair, soap and water for everything else this little place could be a cozy playhouse for you three. This could be a nice retreat for them when I'm working and Maggs is off duty, huh Bry?"

"Sure baby. But, you three listen to me for a minute. Jed said the water down there is deep. There are fish, frogs, snakes and maybe even worse, so when mama and I or Maggs can't go, you can't go, okay? When we can go together, you can go! We'll go today so you can see for yourselves what's there. When we go together you can fish or catch frogs, but the other things down there have to stay down there. Is that clear? Daddy don't want to spank, but he will if you don't listen to that, okay?" Bryen warned looking the three in the eyes.

"Yes sir!" all three chorused.

"Daddy, what's worse than snakes, ugh!" Diego asked.

"Oh a lot of things; alligators, crocodiles to name a few," Bryen answered.

"So, let's go find the broom, buckets, mop and the chair that Ari wants. Babe, if I take Ari with me to the house to gather supplies, can you and the boys drag out the trash and pile it up?"

"We got this babe. Some of this stuff looks like antiques, so we will make several piles. One to burn in the bon fire tonight, and the other to sort through and have appraised, okay?" Bryen told her.

"That's why you are the man; kiss me!" Tawnie said leaning into him. "Be right back guys. Come Ari," and they walked back to the house. In the meantime the guys dragged a broken weaving loom, piles of straw in an old piece of covering that had to have been a mattress, a spinning wheel that spun cotton threads, spools that held the prepared cotton threads, the legs from a hand crafted chair, a perfectly preserved cradle and a chest of some kind.

"Dad, look here," Diego called out. "What's in this?"

"Hmmm. Well pull it outside so we can get a good look son." Diego pulled the chest out, which was almost as large as he was. Miguel helped him and they got it around to the side of the little house.

"Diego, grab that blanket we were sitting on and spread it out please?" Bryen asked his son.

"Yes sir." Diego grabbed the small lunch blanket, Miguel helped him spread it out and the fella's sat down.

"Now boys, this chest looks interesting huh? Check out the scroll work cut into the lid. This is Spanish or Portugese, and I speak Italian so it might take time to translate. *Manter fora!* I think that means keep out. It would make sense, wouldn't it? *Privado!* That sounds like private. So this chest is the personal belongings of someone. Let's see if we can find and translate the name of the owner. *Esta propriedade pretence Enrique`Salvatore.* Ok, it means this property belongs to Henry Salvatore. Well guys that was easier than I thought."

"You did good dad," Miguel told Bryen while holding his hand up for a high five slap.

"We all did good, son. Now to get it open. See this lock? It is ancient, and it's made out of cast iron. Now iron ore came from South America; well it's in the ground everywhere, but the South Americans were able to mine it as no other country before it. I think Africa could but they didn't see it as profitable and went for the diamonds instead. Everywhere we walk there is something of value under our feet, if we just take the time to look for it. This lock is going to be tough. I will have to do some research to find out how to get it open. "

"Dad, maybe that's why it's out here in our little house. No one could open it," suggested Miguel.

"I think you're right son. Here comes mama and Ari so let's put the blanket over top and tomorrow at work I'll do some research. Okay fella's back to work. Hey Babe. You get everything we need?"

"I think so. I'll start with the little window. This must have been added years later because most of the enslaved did not have the luxury of glass windows in their cabins, right Bry?"

"You're right. And the way this little house is positioned, way back off in the distance away from everything else is a clue that whoever lived here was favored somehow. The looms tell me that a lady lived here and must have been the seamstress for the entire plantation."

"She must have been the lover of the master, his son or his brother," Tawnie said. "I wonder if she ever willingly submitted to him or was it a constant taking against her will."

"We'll never know, but to make yourself feel better you might want to imagine that she fell in love with him Tawnie."

"Yeah, I know. I don't want to sink into depression because of what happened probably a hundred years ago."

"Baby, I'm gonna keep you too busy for that. So let's keep working, huh?" Bryen told her.

"Thank you sweetheart. Ari, are you sweeping in there? You're such a good sweeper."

"Yes mama. My house gotta be clean," Ari called from inside. She was just like her mother when it came to cleanliness. She always wanted a duster or broom in her hands.

Several hours later, after breaks for supper, the little family set all the wooden scraps on fire and and enjoyed the night. The fire warmed them and after awhile the little ones started to doze and Bryen hustled everyone inside to bed.

4 CHAPTER

As promised, Bryen researched the lock and methods for opening it and purchased the tools. It would take a pick and a wrench. A local locksmith taught him how at the shop and with practice Bryen knew he could do it with the pirate's treasure lock. He and the children began calling it that though they weren't really sure what was inside. On the day he was ready to try the lock he called the boys to him, they went out to the play house which was spic and span, pulled the chest out, gathered around and said, "Guys this is going to be our secret. We are going to become 'keepers of the treasure' which means whatever we find in the chest must be kept secret from anyone but mama. One day the pirate might come back and want his treasure, but since we are watching over its safety we can get paid a portion of it. So let's take an oath and rub our spit together, because that's how pirates did it. Okay? Diego, what words would you use to seal a bargain between us. Miguel you write down the words and we'll all repeat them, spit and clap hands."

"Ok dad. I say, 'Roses are red, treasures are blue, I keep this pirate secret, and so better you!' How's that?"

"That's great son. Now Miguel can you write all that down?"

"Yes sir. How do you spell treasures?" After getting the correct spelling for the hard words, writing the oath down , repeating it to each other several times, the three spit in their hands and slapped their palms together.

"Okay, just give me a few minutes to unlock this bad boy, and we will celebrate if there's anything good. I brought home some bubbly for all of us, so let's hope we have something to celebrate." Frank stuck the pick in and then the wrench and worked the lock and said, "Wa-la! Now, boys each of you grab a side and on my count of three raise it slowly. One, two, three, up." And inside the chest was unimaginable riches.

"Wow, dad look at all the sparkly stuff," Diego said. "Is that diamonds dad?" he asked Bryen whose mouth was hanging open.

"Looks like money too. Gold money dad. And Diego those are jewelry. Mama has some but her stuff is smaller, huh dad?" Miguel asked Bryen.

"Yep, much smaller." When he could finally speak, he confirmed that Tawnie had nothing like what they were looking at. This was indeed a treasure that could only have come from pirates looting and pillaging ships during Napoleon's day or the Civil War. Perhaps it came from the ship of a blockade runner who was paid to get a plantation owner and his family away from America and didn't make it in time. Maybe Tawnie would know more. "Well guys, to be honest with you, I didn't really believe there was anything in the chest of value. I thought at the most there would be some poor fellows clothes or old boots. But this, this means we have to keep the pirates treasure just between us and the vow is now in effect. We watch over it and use only what we need, right?"

"Right," both boys echoed Bryen. "Only mama; maybe we need to put it back in our playhouse dad to keep it safe," Miguel said.

"I think you're right son. It has sat there for only God knows how long, and stayed safe from thieves, so I think it will be important to put it back. Evidently no one knows about it. Let's take one special piece out to surprise mama. Now, let's see. Which piece of jewelry would you give mama Miguel?"

"Ummm, how about the black bead necklace? What kind of bead is that dad?"

"Those are pearls son. We can look them up in the dictionary then take this piece to the jewelry shop and have the Jeweler tell us how much the necklace is worth. It is a nice piece. I like the cameo on the bottom. See the lady's hat carved in it. This looks like a rare piece and I bet it cost a lot in its day. Diego, do you agree we should give this one to mama?" Bryen asked his youngest son.

"Uh, I like the silver cup, but for a lady I think mama will like the black one."

"Well, take the cup and put it in your room. You can use it for your pencils. When you get ready for college, we'll take it and sell it for your college fund. That means you will be able to go to the big school if you want to, in any place you want to go. But we'll talk about that when you grow up, okay? Now Miguel do you see a piece you'd like to keep in your room?

"How about the ring with the gold lion face on it? It looks too big for me now, but when I get bigger I will wear it, right dad?"

"Yep, you can. As soon as it fits you, put it on but wait until you grow up to wear it or take it out of the house, okay?"

"Okay dad. I like to look at it, that's all."

"Good boy. When you get ready to go to college, you can decide if you want to keep it or sell. Okay, let's go show mama. Ari is too little right now so she won't need anything, but as she grows up we'll let her choose a piece. For now, she'll just see the chest locked up just like we found it."

∞∞∞∞∞∞

That night after dinner, after Ari had been taken upstairs with Maggs to have a bath, the boys and Bryen presented Tawnie with a box. She was excited because she knew the day was not special, so she asked them, "Well guys, what did I do to deserve this?"

Bryen winked at her and said, "Diego, you go first. Tell mama why she gets such a wonderful gift."

"I love you mama. You a good mama."

"Thanks baby. I love you too."

"Okay, Miguel it's your turn," Bryen encouraged Miguel. "Do you want to tell mama something?"

"Mama, we found a treasure in the old house. Dad learned how to open the lock and there was so much stuff in there, and we wanted to share it with you. I got something upstairs, Diego got something in his room and Ari doesn't need anything cause she's too little. When we get bigger we will go to the big school and Ari can have something then, right Diego?"

"Yep!"

"Aww, guys. Thank you both, and thank you Bry."

"Now open it love," Bryen encouraged her.

Tawnie did, and her eyes opened wide at the sight of the beautiful piece of jewelry inside the box. "Oh my goodness guys. To be loved by you guys is wonderful, and evidently rewarding. Thank you all. Come give me a hug and help me get this on. You say this was in the treasure chest?"

"It sure was. Each piece of jewelry lay in a little section of its own and all of it was covered with a cloth. There were little sacks of gold coins, and other jewelry. There's several cups; one of gold, one of silver that Diego has using as a pencil holder, several rings for a man and Miguel has the one with a lion head inset. Pure gold Tawnie. Yes, that looks nice on you."

"It does. One day you'll have to show me the rest, but in the meantime, fellas aren't you two ready to go up now. I am, it's been a long day. One more hug, and I will see you after we come up. Love you."

"Night mama," both boys said. As the boys ascended the stairs, Bryen took Tawnie on his lap, and told her about the chest. "Baby my mouth dropped open when I saw it. I tried to keep my cool, but I could have peed my pants I was so excited. I think it's from the plantation owner, the one who lived here all those years ago. I can only make a wild guess as to why it's out there. What do you think?"

"Oh Bry, my guess would be only as good as yours! Was he preparing to take it to the bank and for some reason he was stopped. Maybe the troops arrived and he was too late. Babe, we'll probably never know. But his lost is our gain, and oh do I love this." And she started twirling around watching her necklace fly out and around her neck.

"It looks good on you. I told the boys the pirate might come back and want his chest of treasure, so we can't tell anyone but you. I even had them write down a made up oath that we took. It was cute. It gave them a reason for keeping quiet about it."

"Did you find a piece for yourself?" she wanted to know. Now that they had it, she wanted them all to have fun with it. If it was all real, they had more wealth than they ever dreamed of.

"Not yet. There is another ring almost like the one Miguel chose except the animal is a cobra with green stones for eyes. They look like emeralds or péridot. I think I might choose that one for myself, but I don't usually wear jewels, you know." As he talked, the necklace Tawnie had around her neck began to glow. The white hat on the lady in the cameo that hung from the bottom became bright, then brighter still and right before his eyes Tawnie began to fade. "Tawnie what's happening?"

"I don't know! I feel alright, but it looks like I'm starting to fade. Oh no, I hope this isn't one of those time travel reactions to a troubled past of someone's life! Bry, if I disappear altogether, know that I love you and have always loved only you. I will fight my way back to you and our babies with everything in me, okay?" and she began to cry.

"I know sweetheart, and know that I feel the same way. If you end up in the year that we think this necklace is from that means you could become somebody's slave, so watch your attitude, show humility and do whatever will keep you alive and well, and know that I support that. Maybe you should snatch the necklace off . . .!" and as he was speaking, Tawnie grabbed the necklace tried to snatch it off and faded completely.

5 CHAPTER

As they suspected, when Tawnie opened her eyes she was in 1863 right smack in the middle of the American Civil War.

She was on a road and troops of the Confederate army were moving past her. Good thing she had on a pretty yellow cotton spring dress, with slippers on instead of jeans and tennis shoes which would have made her stand out even more than she did. She backed up into the tree line and made an attempt at being inconspicuous. She tried to think like a young black woman in the nineteenth century and what changes she needed to make to stay whole and well. She ran her hand through her lightly streaked reddish-brown hair that hung down her back, remembering what the stylist told her about color and perm and knowing that soon both would fade. The natural color would return and so would her waves. Right now she looked more Latina than African but she didn't think slave owners cared what her true identity was; all they would see was the darker tones to her honey colored skin and know she wasn't a pure white woman. She needed a handkerchief to tie around her head because one point she could remember was that unless you were up north, women of color almost always had their hair tied up in a chignon. She bent down and tore the bottom ruffle from her slip, thanking God that it was made of satin and wouldn't be overly hot. As she leaned over to capture her hair inside the makeshift scarf, she heard a voice say, "Well, well, well, what have we here?"

Tawnie completed the job with her hair and stood up tall with her back straight. Whatever happened she would not be that simpering quivering miss who most males of the day expected. If she could catch them off guard, give them what they weren't expecting, they might be too confused to think beyond what they were seeing.

"Mornin gents. How's the war progressin?" she added trying to use the southern drawl of the area. "Ya'll headin anywhere in particular?" She knew she was being bold but she couldn't help it; she would not cower, at least not yet. Let these rebels show her what they were made of first.

"Well now, aint you a pretty one. Who you belong to gal?" the leader asked.

Tawnie suspected this was a man or some rank because he was leading others, had the yellowish gold sash which she knew from Gone With The Wind meant status, so she tried to show him a bit of respect without groveling. "I belongs to Massa Hazelton, General. Might I draw you some wawta, and get yall a bite ta eat?" She knew they wouldn't want to go back the way they had just come, so she pointed in that direction. "We lives just ovah yonda if yall wants ta go backwards."

"Lt. General John C. Pemberton. We just came from that way, so no thanks, but walk with us a ways and tell us about what's been happening around here," the tall olive-complexioned, well spoken southerner stated. "We are headed after the Union supply trains on this road. This is the Raymond-Edwards Road aint it?"

Tawnie knew from her day, in 1983 that there should be a road by that name near their new home, so she made up an answer to the affirmative. "Yes General, yall on the right road. I hear tell from my massa that this the road name. I's watchin fo the young'ens who went fishin for catfish and crawdads. Would love to share a few wit'chall if ya can spare an hour or two." She knew he wouldn't want to hang around waiting so she put her appointment for a time he would not agree to.

"The thought of fresh fish sounds marvelous, but we cannot spare the time, so we'll keep to the road. Watch ya self now, the Yankees are around here somewhere. Forward soldiers!" he called out to his troops.

Tawnie gave a little curtsy and waited until the army moved away before she turned and headed in the opposite direction. Now where to, she thought. Just keep walking and eventually she knew she would meet up with others or come across a plantation, move onto it, pretend she belonged there and wait until she transitioned back to

1983.

As she walked she looked around at the countryside and thought how serene it all appeared, but the truth was an atrocity of the worst kind was occurring not far from where she walked. Brother against brother, father against son, cousin against cousin was causing unimaginable suffering and carnage across not only the south but the north as well. She remembered studying about the Civil War in school and thinking how insane the leaders who instigated the whole event were. How the Devil used humans to turn against each other with such fervor, thinking they would go slaughter, return home and somehow be the same. The truth turned out to be much more terrifying and horrendous than anyone could have ever predicted. At the end, after all was counted, it turns out that it was one of the deadliest wars in American history. As many as six-hundred-twenty-thousand individuals lost their lives, the most before or since. The Confederate army deaths were about two-hundred-sixty-thousand, of which ninety-three-thousand were killed in combat, while Union deaths were three-hundred-sixty-thousand of which one-hundred-ten-thousand died from combat. The major cause of death was disease, which no one could have foreseen except the Creator, and He had no part in it. Men's love of themselves, love of money, inestimable desire for that which was not obtained by the sweat of their own brow, unquenchable greed, lust for power, haughtiness, disloyalty, disagreeableness, fierceness and their being puffed up with pride all led to the downfall of a system that would never be the same. Tawnie tried to push what she knew was coming from her mind and thought about ways that she could possibly change events for the good, even if for only a few.

As she walked she tried to remember everything she knew about black women who were enslaved from books and movies. Females that were of child-bearing age were sold on the market for breeding and were valued for their reproductive as well as productive capacity. So either she could be kept pregnant or kept in the fields. Wow, what a future, she thought. She'd rather have one partner, be kept in the big house as a kitchen assistant, cook, housekeeper or someone who watched over the master's children. Tawnie began to pray silently for direction, hope and more faith. As she did, her stomach grumbled, her mouth watered and she began sniffing the air, knowing she smelled grilled pork. Oh how wonderful it was, especially since she hadn't eaten since, well she wasn't sure how time worked here, but she had eaten dinner with her family and that was the last time. She left the road, and walked toward the smell , ending up at a back gate. She gave a whistle to call any plantation dogs to her, not wanting to catch them off guard, be surprised by her and attack. Since none came, she quietly stepped through the gate and onto the land. She eased her way toward the smell of roasting meat.

"Hello!" she called out not wanting to startle anyone, and glad there were no dogs kept around, because there was nothing worse than a plantation dog. Ugh!, she thought and trembled.

"Yes!" someone called back. Tawnie rounded a magnolia tree and saw the back of a tall woman standing over the stone grill. Turning to face in Tawnie's direction was a middle-aged biracial woman who would probably be called a quadroon here in the south," Tawnie thought. She had few lines in her face, and looked Lena Horne in her 40's. Tawnie had to come up with something, quick.

"Hello there ma'am. I think I'm lost. I'm from Grenada Mississippi and I came to work for the Hazelton plantation as a cook's helper. I was sent by my mistress who heard tell bout extra work needin doin in the kitchens. Do you know how far I has ta go? I'm mighty hungry and tired."

"Well chile, hee hee, you are where you oughta be. This here's the place. I'm Flora, known far and wide as Big Mama. I'm the big house cook so I reckon ya can assist me. Do you have training chile?"

"Yes ma'am Big Mama. I'll be glad to help out and show you what I can do." Tawnie was just glad she could rest and have a meal. She saw a bench at the back of the shelter and asked Flora, "Big Mama, is there any cool water nearby?"

"Of course honeychile! Excuse my manners, I be there directly. Have a seat in the shade. Where ya belongings?"

"The rebels came past me and took everything I had. Do you think I could get a few things from one of the women round here? I didn't have much, but them scoundrels took all there was. They didn't notice my pearls, thank god. They's just a cheap gift from my missus. Course she ain't sharing none of her real stuff," Tawnie lied showing Big Mama her necklace hidden under the collar.

"Those are sho pretty chile. You best keep'em hidden though, cause there's snakes all around here and I don't mean the kind that slithers. These snakes walk up right. The war is driving folks ta do thangs they might not've done befo. And cheap are not, they's take em as quick as ya blinked!" Big Mama said angrily.

"I know that's right! Who lives in the big house, Big Mama? It sure is pretty round here. Everything smells heavenly, not only those ribs or whatever you're cooking but nature itself. Is that magnolia blossoms I smell?"

"Sho is sweetheart! Hee Hee, you like that? We have all variety of trees and bushes round this place. There's fruit trees down in the orchard and roses of every kind in nature. Massa Hazelton's son is a flower and tree expert. They have a name for it, but I can't member now."

"A botanist?" Tawnie suggested.

"That's it! Why missy you sho is smart! What else ya know?"

Over the next hours Tawnie and Flora got to know more about each other and formed a bond. Flora did not have a close relationship with many of the other black women because she was close to the

Mistress and that in itself placed her on a different level in their eyes. Also, Flora was house staff and there was a separation between slaves on all levels of their lives, even down to their color.

When she thought she had built up enough trust between herself and Flora, she told her a few real facts about herself.

"Well Big Mama, I play the piano and teach music. I'm not really from around here. I was born and raised in the north, so I might talk different to you. Big Mama, do you trust me, even though we're still getting to know each other and recently met? I can understand if you don't, but . . ."

"Oh, honeychile, I trust ya sho nuff. There's not many in this world I can trust, but I feel you one that the Lord has sent. Can you trust me?"

"I do Big Mama, why?"

"Young massa and me, we helping people escape to the north. This a station on the underground railroad honeychile. Now you keeps that under yo pretty scarf, ya here?" Flora whispered.

"Of course. The snakes that walk upright that you mentioned, are they living here too?" Tawnie wanted to know exactly what she had to deal with.

"Yep! Right up in the big house. The Ol' Massa is a tryant sho nuff! Ya can't let him know what's going on. He walks around with a gun on his hip and a shotgun by the doh! He's the type of man that eats up the whole earth, and his friends are those that stand round and watch."

"I've heard of those kind. You and I won't just stand round and watch, Big Mama. We are the kind that will take action and stop the others. How do you two manage it? Moving people on and off the property when there has to be some here that are loyal to the Ol Massa. What is the son's name? And what about the Ol Missus?"

"The Ol Missus is a dream to work for. She's the sweetest thang on

God's green earth. Her name is Regina, and she comes from the north too. She's abolition, from a Quaker family and works with us when she can. The son is Henry. He has a ship that he moves families on and takes'em north; sometimes even all the way up to Canada. Would ya like ta meet'em? He'll be back soon. And yes, you right bought a few that would rather die with Ol Massa than lift they hand to help others. I's let you know who they is when they show they faces. One is the obaseer Horace. We got ta watch him," she shared softly.

"I would like to meet Henry, Big Mama. Where is he now?"

"He had to take a small group to the ship, but not to the north yet. He be back soon. I spects him any time now. How the wawta taste? It come from the spring so it's real cool, fresh and good, huh?"

"Yes ma'am. This bar-b-que is good too. And the greens are delicious. Big Mama, is there a small weaving house here, with a loom, shelves full of dyed cotton and spools with cotton wrapped around them?"

"Yes honeychile, there is. And guess what? It's been empty since Reeta died in childbirth. Would ya like to see it?"

"I'd love to. It might just be the place for me to stay and a quiet hideout. I can come and go from there without drawing the attention of the overseer and those who are against the work. If I need to be introduced we can say I come from one of the other plantations, that I'm on loan for just a short time and must go back and forth. They do that down here don't they?"

"A lot of the mens are loaned out that way, yes. Henry or the Ol Masta gives'em a pass. Make sho ya get's one from Henry. Reeta didn't have much, but what's here, a few clothes an such you can have. Here we go; oh good, one of the women been round to clean and get rid of the waste, so it's already to move ya right in. Oh, baby I nevah got ya name. What we call ya?"

"Well, since you've been calling me honeychile, how about Honey? I'm use to it and it's believable. My real name probably wouldn't be."

"Ok, Honey it is. I hear the horses comin, so mayhap it's Henry. Here chile, let me pour wawta over ya hands and use that towel to wipe yo face.   There's a piece a lookin glass to see if ya like what'cha see. Ya dress is pretty, is that the style up north?"

"Thank you Big Mama; yes it's called a sun dress. I can make you several if ya like. I'll need to make myself more clothes anyway. I'll look around in here for supplies if you want to go meet Henry. Oh, and I know this might sound strange but what exactly is the date? I know it's spring, and I know it's probably 1864."

"Not quite. It's May 15, 1863. Rest nah, and I'll bring Henry to ya a little later, " Flora told Tawnie as she left to greet Henry Hazelton, aka Enrique` Salvatore.

6 CHAPTER

While Tawnie napped, Flora fed the family. After making sure they each got dessert, she was finally able to rest herself. On the way out of the dining room, leaving the younger women to clean and put away, she slipped Henry a note telling him that she had a surprise for him, that he would see it later that night after his father and mother went to bed. Flora went to have her own meal and then into her room to rest while Henry spent time with his parents.

Later that night, after his parents were settled in their room on the second floor, Henry went to find Flora. "Big Mama, you ready to get up for the night work?" Henry called and knocked on Flora's bedroom door off the back porch. Henry had a voice that purred and begged to be listened to. It was like the rumble of hot water beginning to boil; deep, soulful, masculine.

"Come on in Henry. Have a seat. Did everything go as planned with the delivery?"

"It did. What's the matter; you still in bed?" Henry asked worriedly. "I thought you'd be up raring to go. You know I wanted to take you with me on the ship tonight."

"Henry, I'm going to stay in and rest these bones for tonight but I got a surprise fo ya out in Reeta's weaving house. Ya has help, just not from Big Mama fo tonight. Gone nah, and see. Let me know tomorrow what ya think. And Henry, take care and go with God."

Henry grabbed, then kissed Flora's tired and worn knuckles. This was one of the hands that tended his bumps and bruises all his life, the hands that smoothed his fevered brow, the hand that gently rocked him when waking from strange and scary dreams, and the hand that was outstretched to him with abiding love, patience, hope and unquestionable understanding when he needed those attributes most.

Flora was given to Marcus Hazelton by his father as a wedding gift to be used as a wet-nurse. At the time, Flora had her own nursing infant feeding at her breast, but nine months later she was told to remove her child and put only the children of the Hazelton's to suck, from then on. Henry was the first child put to her for nursing, and more followed but none lived. After a few years, Marcus thought he would see if children from his seed and Flora would catch and live, because he wanted many children.   So he set Flora up in a cottage about a half-mile from the big house; not too close and yet not too far away from him. He began visiting her at night, had her trained by a French-born chef, and Flora, though she had five sons with her Master felt only contempt for him. She never talked disrespectfully of him to the children though, because she knew men needed another male around to grow up to be men. Eventually the men would see what he was for themselves; she kept her place.

Marcus was thrilled that their sons lived, but none were light enough for him to consider legitimate. He wanted a couple of them that would be light enough to pass for white. Marcus was afraid that Henry would not live long enough to inherit the fortune that he had amassed, and that had been passed to him from father; but thankfully Henry proved to be the strongest of the lot and very healthy. When Henry graduated from the US Military Academy at WestPoint, Marcus began to breathe easier. He decided that yes Henry would live and poured his attention if not his love into him, his only legitimate heir. Marcus did not totally discount his sons by Flora, still putting them to work around the land on duties that brought him profits from their labor. He agreed when asked by Flora to not allow their sons to be put in the "factories in the field", but had them trained in skilled professions that they could take with them in their dreams of freedom. Marcus believed in being a self-sufficient plantation owner and squeezed a penny just as tightly as his closest neighbor. He figured why buy a tool if you had the skilled labor to make one; why buy a board when you had trees that could be cut down from your own forest. So he had one son trained as a blacksmith, one in horse husbandry, a carpenter, a cooper and even one who could tell his father what to plant, where and when to plant it. They were all tall handsome artisans who Marcus treated if not overly harsh, not overly kind either. Marcus was no fool, and knew that harsh treatment would just drive them to want to escape their lots and leave him paying for what he could get for free. Well, unbeknownst to him, his own pure white flesh and blood would act justly even when it was not in Marcus to do so. When the war started, Henry purchased a ship and began moving his brothers off the plantation, replacing them with those who he had trained under his half-brothers tutelage. Henry knew that because his father was oblivious to each of them, they could get away with it. And as long as Flora stayed on the land, there would be no reason to suspect the truth. If or when the tides turned and before the south fell, he would gather Flora up and spirit her away north also. For now, she could work with him on the Underground Railroad freeing as many of the South's enslaved as possible.

As Henry walked out to the weaving house he thought over his conversation with Flora and wondered if she was ailing. She looked healthy, if a little tired, but he saw her bustling around before dinner as she usually did. His mind was on her when he reached the little house and instead of knocking, which he had no reason to believe he had to do he walked right in, and what he saw made his heart stutter and skip a beat. Bent over, pointed toward him as in invitation was the most luscious, shapely, mouth-watering backside he had ever seen. His cock roared to life, stood up, saluted, and wept. A golden-hued woman, was bent down stirring the fire to life, and if she only knew that the heat from his body could do more for her at this moment than any blazing fire, she would move toward him. He could smell that she had just bathed because the air was filled with her glorious, sweet, honey-dew like scent. He felt a swirling, a pulling in his gut like a rip-tide in the ocean. He also felt an intense longing as if he already was about to say goodbye before he even said hello, felt her absence intently.

Tawnie had just stepped out of the tub, dried herself and bent to stir the coals in the fireplace because even though the days were hot, the nights held a chill. She didn't hear the door open while she dried herself meticulously, in and around all her crevices and crannies. While she rubbed the towel over her trim and toned body, she hummed a song from her true time, a song from 1983. She loved the music of Roberta Flack and hummed Killing Me Softly, swaying in rhythm to its beats. She began to sing, take steps, sway slowly and then turned toward the door and saw what she thought was an unknown stranger. She screamed, and Henry threw up his hands harmlessly shouting, "It's okay Miss, it's okay, I'm Henry!"

Tawnie quickly covered herself with the towel and turned her back to Henry saying, " Oh. I didn't hear you Henry. I was expecting Big Mama though. Can you turn around so I can throw something on please?"

"Of course," Henry stated while turning to face the door. He had seen it all so he was okay with turning around now. If this was Big Mama's surprise, he was very okay with it. Where did she come from, he wondered. "Excuse me my dear, I didn't mean to catch you in an uncompromising position. Like I said, I am Henry Hazelton, and I am happy to meet ya. Did you give yo name?"

"You can turn back around now. I'm Honey. If we can get by on just that, call me Honey. I love your home. Big Mama was telling me about how I might help around here, so I told her I can do a lot of different things. I play the piano and taught my old masters children to play and write music. I know that skill is not useful in everybody's home, but I can also assist in the kitchen and the sewing room. I was born up north but was brought down here when my Mistress married a Southerner. Ooh, I feel so much betta after that nap and bath. Thank you for having me around, and I'll do what I can to help you in your duties."

"Wow! I've nevah heard a black woman talk half as much as you do. I find it soothing and rather refreshing and I think it can be useful in calming my friends down when they come to us in need of assistance. Catch my meaning, Miss Honey?"

"I do Mr. Henry. Big Mama told me you might need help tonight. As you can see, I'm ready," Tawnie told him and since she had completed her personal hygiene, she reached out to shake Henry's hand.

"Yes, I do see, but sit down here a minute Miss Honey, please. I'd like to talk just a moment if you don't mind," Henry stated in his deep drawl.

Tawnie looked him over, moving her eyes up and down his tall magnificent frame like a spot light from a light house lamp, not missing a thing, and then back up searching his deep green eyes, and remembered the eyes of the cobra that were on the ring in the treasure chest, and realized that the stones matched Henry's eyes. The treasure was his, she was almost certain. But the name that Bryen said was carved into the chest was Enrique` Salvatore. She knew that Henry in Spanish was Enrique`, but where did the Salvatore come in. The man, this beautiful green eyed pirate of a man, could in fact be Enrique. He was dark enough, dressed the part in black skin-tight pants that opened with buttons and showed every lump and bump in his almost hard, oversized staff that hung between his legs, with a black and white bandana knotted at his throat. His boots were Hessians so all he needed to complete the part was a gold earring in his ear and a scabbard on his hip. This broad-shouldered southern gentlemen could indeed be Enrique` the pirate owner of the chest. Tawnie felt moistness build in her sweet spot between her thighs.

"Now Miss Honey, I don't want to frighten you, but of course I would be a fool if I just allowed ya, without finding out exactly who ya are, to go with me in my nightly business. I know Big Mama approves of ya, but I must question ya first. Do you agree to be questioned?"

Tawnie looked down at the floor and thought about the consequences of trusting or not trusting this man with the truth. The worst that could happen is he would run her off. "Henry, I guess I have no choice but to tell you the truth. I'm not here by choice, but I'm no spy or anything like that. I know that these days of insanity causes everyone to be on edge and throws suspicion on any one new that comes around. I had no choice in coming here Henry. Keep an open mind when I tell you this, but humans don't control everything that goes on in life. There are invisible forces that, I strongly believe, play a part in our lives. Sometimes events that occur here on earth have no explanation. Do you believe that?"

"I do. Look at this war! It makes no sense at all. People who live practically across the road from each other for years are now willing to take up arms and slaughter each other? For what? A deplorable excuse made by insincere men spouting treasonous lies about state's rights? That's the most B. S. I've ever heard. And guess who is the biggest spouter of them all? My father!"

"I know, and believe me when I tell you it doesn't end well, and they will be fighting longer than they think. If I were you, I would gather those I love and get out of here. Go anywhere in the world, but get away from here."

"I wish I could. I can't run away and leave so many who have no one else to help end their suffering. I must stay and see this war to its conclusion. When it's over and freedom comes for those who are deserving of it, then I may leave. Now, as for you Miss Honey, you were saying?"

"I know what's going to happen Henry because I somehow have been transported, transferred, time-warped, whatever you want to call it, moved to this time from 1983."

7 CHAPTER

Henry looked at Tawnie and knew she was telling the truth. She was not the average negro that he knew; fearful, bowed, broken in spirit, trapped with no place to run without help. Before him sat an articulate, knowledgeable, talented, free, proud woman. He didn't even have to add beautiful, because there was no doubt about that, she was one of the loveliest women he'd ever known.

"I believe you. What's your name? Somehow I doubt that it's Honey. I'd be happy to call you Honey, sweetie, baby, my love, whatever you want."

While she smiled that devastating smile that she used unconsciously on men, she stated, "Tawnie is my name. Tawnie Hazelton. Evidently my father's family came from this land. I doubt that we're related, but of course the enslaved were stripped of their identities and were made to take on the Masters name."

"Yes, that's true. If I begin apologizing for every wrong, we would still be sitting here next week. So, Tawnie, I'm happy to meet you. Now, by what means did you time-warp here?"

"My husband and sons found a chest full of jewelry, coins and other valuables in what I believe was this exact little house. Do you know of such a chest Henry?"

"I might. Go on."

"Well one night, after we'd eaten dinner, my family presented me with a black pearl cameo necklace. After my babies were down for the night, my husband and I went for a stroll and as we were talking the cameo brightened and everything began fading. We suspected what was happening so he told me to do whatever it took to get back to him. When I got here, it was in the middle of the day about a mile down the road. I put the necklace under the pillow over on the bed. Do you remember that piece?"

"I do. In fact I just obtained it. You see I take from the rich and help those who have nothing, those who have built the country with their blood sweat and tears. Those who have died under the lash, had their children sold away from them to raise other children, those whose children were ordered never to learn to read and write for no reason other than it might educate them to the truth. The wealth that should have been used to put their children through college, was used to put their owners children through instead. I am an Equalizer of sorts. A self-appointed restorer of opportunities to our darker brothers. Some might call me an abolitionist and others call me a dirty rotten scoundrel to my face. Many on both sides would rather I sit and rot in somebody's prison, but many others would applaud my effort. Either way, it's a dangerous, thankless job but someone has to try. Do you want to share in that, Tawnie? Believe me when I tell you this; you better have your eyes wide open to what you're getting into, because if you don't, you just might have them shut permanently!"

"I understand, but I think that's why I'm here. The real reason I will probably never understand, can only guess at, but while I am here, I will give my time to you Henry, or Enrique` Salvatore; whichever you prefer, right?"

"Correct. I think your family was enslaved here, and we are meant to see that the scales are balanced, at least for your bloodlines. All the people are Hazelton's so it probably doesn't matter which ones we free first, but free them we will. I am a blockade runner, slipping through the lines whenever the situation presents itself. We can leave now and see if this is one of those occasions. We have a cloudy sky tonight so that will make it safer to move along the coast. Look in that basket and see if there's a black cape to cover that bright dress. Wait, I think the dress will have to go. Pull out the trousers and shirt instead. While I turn my back again, change into them, the boots and then the cape."

"Henry, may I ask you a question?"

"Of course. I will assume you have a lot of questions."

"Probably, but one I've been wanting to ask is why is Big Mama still here? I would think she'd been one of the first people you helped to freedom. Is she waiting for someone else?"

" As I understand it, Big Mama wanted to keep the attention of my father away from their children who I have moved. See, Big Mama and my father have five sons together, and because of my father's inhumanity toward them we got them away and moved others into their places. Our father has not even noticed, which proves his lack of feelings toward anyone but himself. Big Mama told me she has never had feelings for the man, but even the worst of men I believe can be shown love and pitied, though they have none to show. So, personally I think she cares deeply for my father after all these years and finds it hard to leave him. Now, I would rather carve out a chunk of flesh, than ever let her here me say that."

"I'll never repeat it," Tawnie told him, holding up her right hand in oath, and they both laughed.

"Okay, ready? Let's go then. We'll move quietly through the forest and when we get down to the water, I'll row us to the ship. I have the yawl, a boat that the hangs from the ship, that I keep hidden."

With stealth, the pair moved through the grounds of the plantation, through the private forest, down a hill toward what sounded to Tawnie like the river. She'd pushed all thoughts of home out of her mind because she didn't want her conflicting feelings to get in the way of finishing what needed correcting in her present. Home was not far away, Bryen and the children would do fine without her for awhile but Henry needed her here.

"Can I hold your hand? I'm a bit nervous," Tawnie admitted. Up till this point, Henry noticed she had been the epitome of calm, and he wondered where she got her fortitude. He still, on occasion had moments of wariness and thought his new friend was very brave. To have time-travelled and not be a trembling mass of bones, he considered to be a marvelous testimony to her human spirit and her belief in a higher power.

"You have the right to be," he told her while reaching for her hand, "but I consider you to be of great courage my dear. Thank you for standing in Big Mama's place tonight. By the way, you can keep the pearls, you deserve them after all you've been through. It may be your way home also, right? Did you wear them tonight?"

"No. I doubt that the time for returning has come. I'm sure there is much to be done before I can even think of returning home. You need me and I'm yours for the time being. Everything else I have put away to be pulled out in its time. Nice boat. How many will it hold?"

"We've put fifteen adults and four children in here in a pinch. I think it would have to be an emergency to do it again, but at the time they had to be moved or left behind. Tawnie, can I ask you about your husband?"

"Of course."

"Are you two very much in love? What will he think about you being away for any time?"

"We are. When we understood what was happening, he didn't panic but went with it, advising me what to do, but asked that I work hard to return to him. He said he was okay with it. We are creative, understanding, open-minded people who have seen and been through our share of living, let me tell you. I think our strong love and commitment to each other is why we were chosen to experience this once in a lifetime adventure. Whatever happens between you and I, know that we will probably only be together for a short time so don't fall in love with me. I'll try not to fall in love with you."

"I like that you said try not to," Henry told her and leaned in and ran his hand up and down her arm, satisfying his need to touch her in some small way. That created an even deeper desire to take her in his arms. He had to stay focused on the mission ahead of them though, so he made himself pull away.

"How far away is the ship anchored?"

"About a mile down the river. We're almost there. Have you ever been on a ship? Some people get seasick."

"I have and I consider myself a "water baby"; a person who cannot be away from water for extended periods. I love all bodies of water, especially sailing on moon- lit nights on a black sea. How about you? Was this act of saving humanity just up your alley, or did you fight against the role of "robin hood" to the enslaved?"

"I was born for the role, my dear. I love being out there testing the limits of my ability against that unseen enemy, pitting my skills against theirs. I love undercover assignations in the night, the sword play, all leading up to an ultimate win or the agony of defeat. So far we are winning, thank God! Now, on board we have four families, six couples, and five children that were sent alone by their parents who did not want to leave just yet. They are committed to their roles of conductors on the Underground Railroad as long as the war last. Tawnie, we are helping some good, faithful, dedicated, god-fearing people. I just wish I had not been born as part of the problem."

"Henry, we cannot help being born, nor can we change circumstances that we were born into, but we can help be a part of the solution once we know there is a problem. Most people keep their heads buried in the sand, and shame on them. I don't think you have anything to regret, but much to be proud of. I know that I'm happy it was your life that I was dropped into. Can you imagine other scenarios? I can, and shudder to think about some of the alternatives. Oh my god! Hold me Henry, please?" Tawnie begged him, just coming to grips with what could have been her outcome."

"Now, now, stop letting your mind go down those paths. You have come so far, and you were doing so well. Hush now, hush my beautiful traveling angel," he crooned to Tawnie in his deep southern drawl, while she sat shaking and quietly crying in deep sobs, just now coming to the realization of being a young black woman during the Civil War. Henry drew her into his broad chest and wrapped her inside his tree limb thick arms; arms that had wielded swords and sliced men into. Arms that reached out and sheltered children of the enslaved, and tenderly held and rocked their babies in order to keep the train moving to freedom. He rubbed up and down her back, pulled back the hood of the cape to see all of her, and opened the cape she was wearing. He moved her to one thigh, unbuttoned her shirt and began licking her neck and her chin and kissing her mouth. Then, working his way down he gave special attention to his favorite part of her face by sucking on her droopy, pouty lower lip and moved down to each of her breasts, slowly and tantalizingly pulling each over-ripe almond colored nipple into his mouth. Not wanting either one to feel jealous of the other or left out, he grabbed them together and worked both together, shoving them hungrily into his mouth. Tawnie stopped crying and began moaning in ecstasy. She threw back her head, shook out her hair and arranged herself closer to him so that he could get to her easier. His mouth felt so good on her heated body; the moistness of it leaving a trail for the cool air to kiss. He was making her so excited she wanted to tear off her clothes and have him take her right here inside the little canoe. It would be terribly uncomfortable, unless . . . "Henry, pull your cock out, and let me straddle you please. I can't stand this sexual tension a moment longer!" she admitted feeling frustrated and unsatisfied.

"You ain't said nothing but what I've been longing for since I walked into the cabin. I am at yo command my precious angel," Henry gasped out unevenly. He reached for her pants and helped pull them off, saying, "Oooh, no under things? How convenient for my Ol Hickory," he said as he pulled his cock from a hole in front of his trousers. "I don't know what you're used to but I'm rather large so hold on and bite down on my shoulder if I hurt you when I plunge deep inside that sweet poonanny."

Henry lifted Tawnie and adjusted her hot juicy poonanny over his bulging throbbing over-sized head, and slammed her down on it. They both bit down on each other's neck and were able barely able to muffle the noise that erupted out of their mouths. It would have been screams of pain mixed pleasure, but was grunts instead. After they recovered from the shock of the entry, they rocked and rode each other until the river splashed over the side of the yawl, wetting them both. Regardless, it was one of the most unusual couplings that either had ever experienced. Notwithstanding the dangerous circumstances, the enemy around the bend, the thrill of the setting under a quarter moon, cool breeze, rocking canoe and a gorgeous partner, all of it made for their pleasure. The two of them wanted to give of themselves but they also wanted to receive the pleasure that came from the other because who knew when it all might abruptly come to an end.

Henry spoke first saying, "Oh my dear. I knew you would be delicious if you ever let me in, and I was right. Thank you for allowing me to partake of such lusciousness. And forgive me for the pain. Can I help you button up, we are just about to come upon the port side of the ship.

"I'm ready. Wow! I think that drained every bit of energy I had left. Now all I want to do is curl up and sleep for a week. Henry, you do have a place of your own on the ship, right?"

"Yes, Tawnie angel. I have a nice private patroon fore cabin away from everyone. It's designed for occasions like we just shared, or to sleep the sleep of Lazarus. How about we climb aboard, you go right to bed and I'll let the crew know to head to the Caribbean. Tomorrow we can see where we are and I'll introduce you to the families."

"Sounds wonderful. I'm too tired to do any talking or smiling. It's been a long day."

Henry gave a signal; the one the crew knew meant drop the ladder so he could climb aboard.

8 CHAPTER

Tawnie fell into sleep as soon as her head hit a pillow that was unusually soft for the year 1863. She assumed it was specially made for some rich land owner and obtained by Henry under "special circumstances", as was most of the treasure. Before sunrise she felt the mattresses sink under the weight of Henry and automatically turned into his side to be held. Since she was eighteen years old, she had lain next to a man. First Rico, Bryen's brother. Then Bryen her husband, and now Henry; so when he finally came to bed, after taking care of his cargo and crew, handling the helm for a few hours, it felt normal to tuck her head under his chin and throw her leg over his thigh. Whoever owned the bunk previously was a big man, because when she was alone, it swallowed her, but now that Henry arrived it was the perfect size.

Henry was just as tired as Tawnie was, but he was also horny after getting a taste of her exquisiteness earlier. He was naked and let himself be her pillow for a few minutes, then he began rubbing his hand up and down her body. When he turned her over onto her back she opened herself up for him, and he worked his way from her head to her toes, sucking and licking his way down. Then he started back up, pausing when he got to her hairy mouth and use his tongue to batter and thrash her clitoris, urging the shy raisin sized nub to poke it's head out. When it did he caught it between his lips and pummeled until Tawnie practically levitated off the mattresses. She wrapped her legs around his head and softly squeezed while rocking his face into her moistness. He lapped up her juices like a kitten with a bowl of milk, and when she reached the stars, began laughing and writhing beneath him, screamed into a pillow, Henry knew it was time to go to work. He turned her on her stomach and entered from behind. She crossed her ankles, he sat on her thighs and she became his mare. He rode her to the races, won the trophy and rode back to the starting gates. After kissing the back of her neck, plunging deep a couple more times, he leaned back his head and hollered out his explosive orgasm. After he came, he rolled over and went to sleep, and Tawnie thought, just like a man. No matter what year it is, men were the same when it came to hot love making and sleep.

Of course the snoring rattled the rafters, so she put the pillow over his face. When that didn't quiet the snores she got up, washed off their juices and dressed. Wearing the pants and shirt, she grabbed the cape, went up topside to walk around the deck to feel the breeze and watch the sunrise. It was glorious. One second it was completely dark and the next the sky burst forth with rays of yellowish-orange against a background of purplish-blue. She knew at this moment that there was a Creator.

Slowly the entire heavens lit up for another beautiful day of weather, if not peace toward all men. Whatever individuals chose as their happiness for that day, she knew that the Devil was busy and would try and ruin it, therefore the war would go on. She would choose to help the families on this ship, whatever that might mean. She would quietly follow Henry's lead and do whatever it was that a conductor of the Underground Railroad did to lead the passengers to their destination, which in this case was to freedom.

As she walked from bow to stern, Tawnie noticed how immaculate everything was. The crew were quietly performing their duties, but they all bowed to her in greeting and respect, as she slowly passed. The crew were multi-racial and multi-cultural, which made for a more comfortable atmosphere. There was no tension that she felt, but an air of self-determination or autonomy, companionship and brotherhood. Each man worked not for himself alone, but for the good of all. If the group was successful then the individual was also a success. There was no supercilious grandiose attitudes, but humility and fellow-feeling. She looked off the starboard side and saw porpoises jumping high in the air, showing off for her. She gasped and turn to the crew and pointed. While she laughed, she called out, "I think the children should watch this show of a lifetime! Where are they? Can we bring them out to see this?"

"Sure ma'am! Most everyone's still sleeping that's all. Go down those steps two levels and follow the hallway. At the end is a door. Knock twice and whoever is awake will let you in. You can ask the parents and the guardians if they'd like to send the children up with you or come up when they're all ready at the same time. We are far enough out of the danger zone that everyone can breathe easy for awhile. By the way, names Guillermo Santiago. I'm the boatswain, which means I keep the equipment sharp and ready to be used. Let any one of us know if you need anything, and welcome aboard ma'am."

Tawnie curtsied, smiled and said, "Thank you, sir," and hurried down to find the passengers. When she got down to the door as directed, she knocked twice, and said, "Hello. Coming in," and she walked in to the cabin. Inside she found several women and most of the children that Henry mentioned. "Well hello there. My name is Honey, and I work with the Captain in his railroad work. Might I take the children on deck to watch the whales and dolphins play? Though you're all invited."

"Yes ma'am, that'd be great if ya could. I been up most of the night wit the little'uns. They's afraid, never been on a boat and they mama's and papa's stayed behind. My names Eva, and that's Lana. I have two of my own and she has one. Thank ya."

"Nice to meet you Eva, and you Lana. Why don't you lay back down, and I'll see to the children. Come up when you're ready. Just follow the hallway to the ladder and climb up. You'll probably hear us before you see us. I'll get them fed and bathed, and I'll ask the crew for some clothing, so don't be surprised if you find the children in crew clothing which is white pants and white shirts, with a blue sash. Have a nice rest."

Back on deck Tawnie monitored the children while they enjoyed the show. High flips, curls, spins and dives, and the ultimate splash into the faces of the little ones brought forth giggles and squeals from them. The squawked and squealed and shook their fingers at the sea life as if telling them to stop would bring about the desired orders. Tawnie laughed and had a good time as well. The cook directed them all to sit near his doorway to the galley. He served each child a bowl of turtle stew with a hoecake brought from Big Mama's kitchen by Henry. One positive characteristic of riding his train, was the fact that he was a son of plantation owners and could stock the larders well. His passengers would eat hardy, wholesome foods and not the usual slave foods of hardtack infested by weevils and other nasty pest. Big Mama's conductorship role required her to bake, roast meats, collect fresh vegetables from the private gardens and send her collections with Henry, or on nights she could get away to help, stock the ships galley shelves herself.

Tawnie was about to ask if she should go and collect all the other families when they made their way to the deck from below. She introduced herself to them and helped feed them from the galley. After the children finished their meal, she led them on a tour of the ship to get them out of the adults way and to give them a time to continue being children. She encouraged them to run around playing tag, and she marked out a hopscotch game with pieces of material that looked like chalk. After about an hour, the adults joined the children so Tawnie asked Guillermo if anyone played an instrument so she can get everyone to sing. Music was not only a healing source but had a calming influence too. He told her that there were several mouth organs, drums, fiddle and a set of bagpipes aboard. So, she called out the musicians and everyone came together to sing and dance, whoop and holler and just enjoy the freedom that being onboard the ship allowed them.

Tawnie taught them several new songs that could be sung combining just the rhythms from the instruments available. Any thing missing could be improvised or left out entirely. Because she was a graduate of Julliard's College of Music, she was talented enough to write songs on the spot. The crew joined in and they celebrated until Henry came on deck yawning and stretching. "Morning everyone," he said trying to wake fully. "Thank you for that lovely serenade," he acknowledged having heard all the noise going on above his head. "I think I'll go get some coffee or tea. Would you all like a cup?"

There was a chorus of yes sir's aimed at him in response.

"I'll help you Henry," Tawnie volunteered following him a step down into the galley. "How'd you sleep? You still look tired, but I hope me not being there let you sleep unencumbered. I would have wrapped myself around you like a sheet, and you definitely would not have slept well."

"Um, that sounds tantalizing. Let's try it tonight once we get to where we're going. Did you get enough rest?"

"Well, let's just say I also sleep better without the maleficent rafter trembling accompaniments."

Henry threw back his head and laughed heartily saying, "In other words my snoring sounded like a roaring lion, you got scared and scrammed?"

"Yes something like that," Tawnie laughed holding her stomach. Back home, Bryen purred in his sleep more like the little cat, so she slept like a baby, but lying next to Henry all she could do was toss and turn so she got up rather than disturb his sleep. "I might need ear muffs, or something to stuff in my ears if we are going to continue sleeping together."

He winked at her, looking at her intently and said, "Well, we don't have to sleep, but I want no other in my bed but you. I think we can work something out, don't you?"

"Oh, si senor, Enrique`," she said tauntingly with her well known seductive smile. She slipped her shoulder out of its sleeve, and moved it down her arm, freeing up her neck and almost baring her full left breast. Henry moved toward her and captured the bare area in his mouth and groaned as he licked and sucked his way down to her nipple, which was now barely covered. He pulled on the top and chemise and bared it all the way. He began by nipping it with his teeth, and when Tawnie yelped, he drew on it like a greedy baby on its mothers tit, and pulled it all the way in his mouth. She rubbed her body up against his front and felt his huge throbbing staff grow and stretch, wanting to come out and greet her with a nod. She asked him, "Can you make up an excuse or do you have to see to the crew? If you can get away, estare` esperando por ti desnudo!" And to add emphasize to her bold statement, she stuck out her tongue and wiggled it at him like a snake and ran out of the galley.

"Hot damn woman!" Henry called out after her. Then he summoned the boatswain with a shout, "Guillermo! Venga aqui` por favor!"

"Si Senor? What can I do for you?" Guillermo asked Henry deferentially.

"Guillermo, I need a few more hours of sleep. Do you mind passing the coffee pot around and make sure that if the ladies want tea, there's plenty to go around. Thank you for all you do, and get someone to help you if you need it. I'm sure one of the women served in the big house on the land they come from. It might help relax them, if they're given little tasks to perform so the time won't move so slowly for them. If I fall back to sleep, call me around four. Muchos gracias, mi amigo," Henry called over his shoulder with a wave and hurried back to his cabin and to a naked waiting Tawnie.

∞∞∞∞∞∞

"So, sweetheart, who taught you to speak Spanish?" Henry asked Tawnie as he stood before the bunk slowly undressing.

"I grew up around Latino's, Italians, French and mixed races all my life, and in the twentieth century the education system is set up with required courses and extra curriculum, which language was a part of. My sisters and I took advantage of it and chose music and language as our extra activities. What about you, Don Enrique`?" she purred playfully getting on her knees and stalking toward him like a hungry cat after a canary. Henry watched her behind wiggling from side to side and he grew exponentially. When she got to the edge of the bunk, his long dong jumped up out of his trousers and slapped her across the face. She grabbed it and stuffed it in her mouth. Henry's answer to her question flew out of his head and was replaced with inestimable pleasure. His eye bucked, he threw back his head and roared, in part play acting, and part thrilling gratification. She deep throated him, swallowing all she could like a pro. After she drained him, licked up the dribbles, only then could he come up with clear comprehension.

"Mamacita, donde has estado toda mi vida? Little mama, where have you been all my life?" he asked, astounded. "And what did I do to deserve you?"

"Hen-ry! You know what we said about our time together. Let's enjoy each other while we have the opportunity, but seek one who will remain by your side forever. Have you ever been married or engaged?"

"To tell you the truth, my desire is for black flesh. I didn't want to "eat where I shit", pardon my expression, so I didn't take what was right in front of me. Many do of course, but for some reason I want to give the lady I share intimacy with the opportunity to love me and living under the "peculiar institution" it just never happened. Until now. I know, I know! I will keep looking for my forever lady, " he said pouting.

9 CHAPTER

The night was cool and the ship moved closer to its destination, closer to freedom for the enslaved. Some of them had never been free, but had been born to serve at the command of a Government that colluded in the stalking, ensnaring, kidnapping, raping, branding, burning, hanging, brutalization and forced labor of millions of children, women and men. The Government did not care about age, nor gender, nor size. It did not care about culture or religion. If you were male you were used as mules in the fields to grow cotton, tobacco, rice and sugarcane. You were used to drain mosquito infested swamps for irrigation purposes, build dikes to hold water and sluices to drain it off. You carved out forests by cutting down the trees, and used the wood in building everything from outhouses to dining tables. You claimed the fields by removing boulders large and small, and cultivated the ground from which you came in order to plant anything that would grow, saving the weeds to feed your family. You bent your backs building roads, bridges, court houses where you found no justice, office buildings where you could not work, colleges that you and your children could not attend to get an education, and even The White House where the President of that nation's Government sat on furniture built by you or your kin. Not only did the enslaved build his furniture, they cooked his food, designed and tailored his clothing, and laundered them. In fact he was even washed by and shaved by one with a razor held to his neck.

If you were female you were used to cook for, clean for, launder for, seamstress for, and act as nursemaid for the mistress of the big house. You might be assigned duties as a lady's maid, chambermaid, and milk cow for her babies. You had your babies snatched from your breasts to have a masters child placed there to feed. And that night after their child sucked your breasts dry, his daddy supplanted him and sucked from them too. He was there not at your invitation but in spite of your refusal. He took what you did not offer, and planted his seed in your womb, to be subjugated from the cradle to the grave, and then the cycle was repeated. And when that seed sprouted and you gave birth to his offspring, he did not care that it was half white, he put his boot on its neck just as quickly as he did the pure black one.

You planted, harvested, hoed, and the food you prepared for the family, you were not allowed to eat. If you roasted a hog, your man, brother, father or son butchered it, but you ate what was considered the waste, the garbage part of the meat and made something good out of it or starved. They ate the prime choice cuts and let their dogs eat from their plates.

All the work you did was done to make your master comfortable, and the skills you used, the sweat that poured into your burning eyes, the blood that dripped from your cut bodies made him rich. Your labor cost him nothing. But made his bank account fat. And when he died, fat and grey having sucked the life out of you like a greedy leech, you buried him.

Henry told the story that night of watching generations of his family take and take and take from those that were legally theirs. Legalized slavery, so there was nothing he could do. Until a few reasonable normal human beings stood up and said enough is enough. Then they began spiriting the enslaved, the oppressed away to freedom, and without them, there would be no Underground Railroad. And Henry wanted in. So, he donned a new persona and became the pirate Enrique` Salvatore. From those who took, he would take and return some of the gains back to those to whom it belonged. He could not do much, but the little he could do, he promised that it would make a difference. That night, the people on board the ship Tren de la paz (Peace Train) pledged allegiance to the movement; the slow movement of the train cars on the Underground Railroad. They would shine the spotlight on injustice by removing the victim, and help them build new lives where they could be human again. In celebration, Tawnie wrote and shared the words of a new song with them, a song called 'Victory'. She sang,

"Born from the dust, to a couple who could see,

That life had no meaning, unless you were free.

A hard road to travel, not straight but filled with turns,

Follow them you will, because inside you it burns.

Made equal by our Creator, the one who has the sight,

To see we won't be trampled, but fight for what is right!"

That night while Tren de la paz sailed quietly through warm waters of tropical Caribbean, couples strolled the deck, musicians took up their instruments to try and come up with a melody that would work well added to Tawnie's words to complete her song. Children who had been allowed to run and play all day were now sleeping. Their guardians felt more comfortable leaving them alone in their cabins, so they strolled together trying to come up with their own lyrics to make the song more enjoyable. Everyone was excited to be near their destination and to be out of the bloody conflict between the states. Many of them knew that what was said about stated reasons for war was a lie. They wished no one harm, but they also wanted no part of nor supported either side, because in their eyes, killing was never justifiable.

Tawnie and Henry were in the ocean swimming. Because of their daytime antics they both agreed it was time to wash, and what better place than the open sea. Because they were near equatorial boundary's, the water felt better than a tub, and with no constraints of movement they were able to dive and leap up like the creatures she had watched play earlier. Just as Henry started to reach out his arms for Tawnie, he caught a glimpse of a bright light flashing a signal of some kind. He stopped and stiffened and called out to her, "Honey, look there!" and pointed where he'd seen the flashing.

She turned her body in the direction he pointed and said, "I see it. From this far away it's impossible to tell who or what, isn't it?"

"Yes. We won't take any chances. Since we can't fly, we must run and quick!" He gave a loud whistle, his signal, and the ladder came down. They climbed aboard and Henry rushed to the helm to turn Tren de la paz with the wind at her back, darkened her and directed her sails to be hoisted. They took off closer inward to cling to the coast, looking for a place to shelter until the battle ship, which is what Henry suspected it to be drew farther away.

They sailed liked the wind all through the night, and finally found a sheltered cove to spend the day in, and an exhausted pair finally trudged off to try and get a few hours of rest as streaks of pink appeared, and the sky began to brighten. Before they left the deck, giving instructions to spend this day resting and fishing to friends and crew, they looked up to the heavens and watched the glorious beginnings of a new day. Henry drew Tawnie into his arms and gave her a kiss that was so passionate and full of longing that her toes actually curled. Then they moved forward into their cabin.

Whether it was lust or love, he didn't yet know, but what Henry knew was that the excitement of escape heightened his desire for sex, so he reached for Tawnie, pulling her into his physically powerful arms. She pressed her body against his, not wanting any room between them and breathed him in. His scent, the male aroma of him, even his sweat sent delicious spirals of desire raging to her vulva and her body began to produce the wetness it would need to lubricate her walls against his stallion-sized shaft that she knew would pummel and batter her to climax. Under cover of darkness, they had been swimming in the nude, so he reached for her still exposed "mound of Venus" , lay his palm flat against it and began moving it in a circle in order to increase stimulation, lubrication and prepare it for his insertion. He could feel that it was working, as Tawnie shifted against him, being pulled under the spell of his seduction. As they continued standing, she restlessly moved her legs open and closed not sure what to do as her body increased in excitement preparing itself to be thoroughly and vigorously ridden by Henry. He knew she wasn't ready quite yet, so he tongued her lips, running his over and under, inside and outside, finally capturing hers and sucking on it. Then he pulled on her nipples, pinching them between his fingers, and they stretched out to him, longing to have him nurse from them. He acquiesced, leaned down and tugged first one, then the other, then both into his greedy mouth. She writhed against him, and he knew she was almost ready by the hungry sounds she made. Her eyes rolled back into her head, and she flailed from side to side her hair swinging with each movement. He reached up to pull on her hair, to help ground her and hold her still, while he again checked her readiness. This time he used his middle finger and inserted it inside her hairy mouth and made her gasp out loud. While that finger went seeking the treasure buried deep inside, his colossal thumb found and swirled around her hidden turtle that had yet to come out and greet its playmates. He let thumb and turtle play and she pleaded with him deep in her throat. Then he slid his ring finger into her pretty brown flower, the one that held the secrets to how much she could really take from him, and how much she was willing to give of herself. She temporarily stiffened against him, then relaxed and leaned a little forward to help ease his way. She wrapped herself closer, to help regain composure and to push her breasts into his chest since his concentration was elsewhere. She grabbed his rod, softly rubbing her way up and down, tapping the head close to the tiny hole. That got his attention. They fell together onto the bunk and lay intertwined, each trying to get on top. He help her sit on his thighs, she positioned herself and found her true saddle position, and rode him. They both even whinnied and laughed; her because of her frenzied orgasm rushing in on her, and him because he was ardently satisfied and for once, happy.

10 CHAPTER

The entire day was used for rest, relaxation and play. Henry knew none of the families had ever been able to have more than half a day at a time for themselves, without someone in authority calling them back to work. Henry could not imagine living under that kind of persistent pressure and mandatory compliance. To get ready to bathe and have even that interrupted, was inhumane and intolerable. To not be able to sleep when you were tired, and awaken and rise at your leisure, unimaginable from his standpoint. To have the person you wanted to make love to, be forbidden to you was heartbreakingly cruel.

So, that is why Henry strapped on guns and a sword, took to the oceans, played the pirate, took what he thought could be used by his new friends and donated to the cause. He had no time to choose a mate for himself, and for that matter who would he choose? What he desired most was forbidden to him in his own setting. In order to find the woman of his dreams, other than the one who lay next to him, he would have to travel the seas to other nations where marriage to whomever he wanted was legal. He would arouse suspicion if he went to the islands and not state his purpose immediately. He knew there were many of all races who moved around to foreign lands to seek out that which went against nature, but he wasn't one of them. He was a normal red-bloodied male who wanted someone to love, but during these days filled with hate, he had to put away his will and do what was right, do what he could to help others.

As he yawned and stretched he watched Tawnie sleep. He had kept her up most of the early morning trying to get satisfaction, but every time he climaxed and rested for a few minutes, the desire rose up in him again, and he had to have more of her. She was his drug, and he knew it was wrong but he was becoming addicted. My lord, what have I done, and what will I do? He thought about how she had come to be here, in his time of 1863. And he remembered that at any moment she could be gone. In the blink of an eye, lost to him, never to return to this place that he had to stay in. That realization caused him much anguish because if he had a choice, he would not stay. It was useless to continue this line of thinking, he had to get hold of his thoughts. He was no kid in the bloom of youth, but a man full grown at thirty. He looked again at Tawnie, at her curves under the sheet, and knew he would soon want her again. He put his head in his hands and realized that his want would never end, because with her he had found that one soul on earth that he had a commonality, in spite of all their exorbitant differences. This is what he had been searching for all his life, and now to be told that it was all a mistake, a temporary freak occurrence, a once-in-a-lifetime event. "No!" he shouted into the room.

"Ah, what? What happened?" Tawnie jumped awake in fear.

"So sorry, sweetheart. I spoke my thoughts aloud, go back to sleep. It's not time to rise yet. Today we relax, tomorrow we may have to fight." And he reached under the sheet to draw her closer to his body to draw her heat to himself, to imprint her scent, the feel of her on his conscious, to keep the memory of her, if not the reality of her with him forever.

Tawnie returned to a dreamless sleep. And Henry quietly wept.

∞∞∞∞∞∞

Later that day, after everyone had eaten lunch, they all gathered together to discuss plans for the families once they reached the islands. A few of them had relatives already there, thanks to Henry and a few others working the Railroad. Before the war began, the conductors had been moving passengers along the line, mostly to the American north, Canada and even back to Africa for a few. Some feared staying where the hand of the US government might reach and they wanted as far away as they could possibly get. Laws against people of color changed so frequently that it was normal to be leery of putting trust in not only them, but anyone working for the government. Henry traveled wherever his passenger felt more comfortable going. After this trip he would return to the plantation to see where he was needed. He hoped that Tawnie was meant to stay a lot longer and help him, because he had fallen, hard. Lord help them all.

While most of the women were casting their fishing lines from the side of the yawl a few yards from the Tren de la paz, the men sat on board discussing their futures with Henry, Guillermo and the crew. Henry was asking, "Walter, you have your parents and a brother on one end of the island chain. What work will you choose to do?"

"Through messages I got from the Underground, I know my daddy and brothers have cut through the forests and cultivated some parts of the land. Daddy put in crops for local people to harvest and share. There's corn, gourds of all types, wheat, beans, and other plants meant for food. I might farm. Mae-Rose rather me work with the animals that are there. Last trip some of the conductors dropped off horses, cows, sheep and goats, hogs, and chickens. So it's still up in the air as to what I'll do," answered Walter, one of the men who has been enslaved on Henry's land.

"William, do you have anyone there yet?"

"My mother's brothers are there. She had three, one ran before he could be helped. But the other two have gone ahead. Word is they have a small lumber mill on one of the islands and are cutting through the forest, trading the logs and building for themselves and others. I think I will continue to act as a carpenter since that's what I know. I worked at it for Ol Massa Johnson on his land. He loaned me out at week end to others and let me keep a few coins."

"Sounds good, William. Roscoe, what have you chosen to do?" Henry asked a tall, solidly built crimson-toned man who was sent down the line.

"I think I can make a little money at fishing, crabbing, shrimping, diving for pearls and any other thing that comes out of the sea. I loves the wawta, and wants to stay near it if possible. Ya think I might make a go of it doing that, Sir?"

"Yes, the possibilities are endless. There are a significant number of creatures in the seas that we have not even begun to pull out and eat. Good choice Roscoe. If you trade with some, sell some and keep some for your family, you will do very well," Henry acknowledged.

"Luther, you were a laborer in the rice fields for us. Are you thinking of doing other jobs or sticking to what you know?"

"Sir, if I nevah see another rice field it will be too soon. I want to rest for a good year away from any field work. I think I works at trapping and snaring wild birds and other wild life. I hears there are lots of em moving around in the forests that others are cutting through. I knows how to make trousers and moccasins that the natives wear. I sets up a shop and we all dress like the natives. My sons will need work as they grow, so we won't take all life but leave plenty for the days ahead. I was taught that by the Cherokee. Some of them my people on my daddy's side," Luther admitted.

"I think you are on to something Luther. Congratulations for seeing beyond today and into the future. You'll do well," Henry leaned over to shake Luther's hand and slapped him on the back.

"Now, who worked in the forge making and repairing tools used on either our land or other plantations?"

One man, almost six feet tall and obviously with at least one white parent because of his fair complexion and silky locks, stood up and admitted that he was a skilled copper and blacksmith, trained by those who were educated in the craft and passed that training to him. Not because of any benevolence on their part, but because of who his Master/grandfather was, Thomas Jefferson. He stated, "My name is John Christopher Jefferson. The true-hyperbole was that my grandfather freed my grandmother and her children upon his death. The real truth was he did not. My grandmother Sarah was moved to Virginia and sold to her master and lover's relative, where she and her children including my father were kept slaves, working at artisan labor, but unpaid labor it remained. The only gift my grandfather left my father and his siblings was a request in his will that they and any offspring, such as myself, be allowed to remain out of the fields, kept from being used as beasts, and allowed to remain in Virginia. Other than that, we were included in the roster of possessions, just as the animal stock were. The only material possession was to my grandmother to be passed down, a gold pocket watch with an inscription on it that said 'To my Midnight Lady, S always yours, T J' which my master/relative tried to keep before I beat his ass to get it back, and had to get away before they hung me. Not that all of this has anything to do with your question, sorry. Sometimes I do ramble. I did want to thank you for allowing me to come along though, you probably saved my life. As I started to say I am also a blacksmith, skilled in working iron ore so I would appreciate the opportunity to build a forge on a piece of ground I can call my own. I'll use my talents to craft tools and all farm implements needed by our people to work the land and for other jobs as needed. I also play and teach violin."

"Thank you. Do we call you John or Christopher?"

"I think we better use Christopher. My middle name wasn't written down in the paperwork passed to the Virginia family. So I'm safe using it."

"Well, it sounds like you will all have a good start in building a new and wonderful life in the Caribbean, and you can make it what you desire, not what someone else requires. For now, let's go see what our women folk have pulled out of the sea. I'm hungry," Henry laughed, rubbing his belly. And all the men either jumped or dove in from the railing of the ship.

11 CHAPTER

That night everyone gathered on the beach of the hidden cove to eat grilled fish, crabs, shrimp, native fruits and a few items brought from the ship. Couples wandered away gradually and found secluded spots to snuggle in, and children ran wild for their last night with Tawnie, who chased them. It helped kept her mind off missing her own little ones to have others to laugh with, and love on.

Tonight, while the children slept, Henry would pull out and head for the islands of the Caribbean. He would disembark and help offload the passengers, then turn around and return to Mississippi. He'd have to see his father, endure his facile attitude, his smug and sometimes obtuse reasoning. Especially when it came to allowing Henry to handle his share of the responsibilities on the land. But he knew his mother would be waiting on him; as a son he had a duty to her, and he would be happy to see her and of course Big Mama.

The Ravenel House was an eleven hundred acre plantation that sat on a hill surrounded by a valley filled with orchards of every kind of tree imaginable. There were apples, peaches, pears and more. There was a grove of trees that bore nuts of a wide variety too. And of course, like all plantations there were acres of fields of every crop that could grow in the warm climate of Mississippi. The land was very rich and produced bumper yields annually of not only crops to be used for food locally and sold, but most of all humans. At one point there were eleven hundred enslaved humans on the land, those who had no say in their lives, no say in their children's lives. The elder Hazelton men had long been in the business of growing, harvesting, and selling humans just like their crops and animals; and honestly it brought richer gains and fatter bank accounts. For several generations it had been this way; until now. The arguments between Henry and his father were attributed to what his father saw as virtual treason on his son's part, and definitely villainy on the part of the old man, Henry proclaimed. Many times they almost came to blows, and would have had not the wife/mother stepped in and begged them to stop and let it go for another day. Henry now lived on the land, but on the back part of the plantation in a three room cottage. Daily he was seen by the people, they still took care of him as when he was a child in the big house. They brought his meals or stayed and cooked for him in his home, and then left. He had his laundry picked up and taken to the central plantation wash house to be done by the women, as they had always done. So, he participated in the institution of slavery, though he hated it and sometimes hated himself. If he were psychoanalyzed, this would be found as the main reason he remained single.

If his father took an actual count of his people, he would find that more than half of them were missing. Not only was this attributed to the war, but also to the efforts of Henry and the work of the underground. Somehow, with the acumen of a genius the fields were being harvested, the household duties were being done, the animals were producing and being taken care of, and some were attributing it all to miracles. Many prayed that before the truth was revealed, before the Old Master had connected the dots, they too would be gone to the promised land.

∞∞∞∞∞

Three days later, without running into any war ships or other threats, the Tren de la paz anchored in its usual place and the crew let down the yawl, and then Henry and Tawnie. After dark, they made it back to land, passing the way they had come several weeks before. Henry walked her to the old weaving house and let her know that he'd be back later that night, kissing her deeply. He went up to the big house to face his father.

"Mother, how are you dear? You know I missed you this trip," Henry held his mother, expressing his true feelings.

"Well son, I missed you more. How was the trip? You look rested, evidently you had a day for yourself?"

"Yes, mother. I took two days to rest. I had to. There were war ships on the ocean, but I ran and didn't see which side. Of course it didn't matter, considering the cargo we carried. You look well. How do you feel?"

"I'm well son. I've tried to direct the staff as you would want me to. I had a visitor. I had to tell the conductor to return next week because you were already on the tracks."

"Wonderful! Thank you. Where's father?"

"In his study with the Thornton brothers. They want to purchase several house servants for their place and a few of the thoroughbreds. They're also planning a small competition between the horses they brought and several they want to purchase, and want your father to host it here. What do you think of that, son?"

"Hmm, well if he's partying, he won't be wondering what we're up to, but I think it would attract too much attention from other quarters. Don't they realize there's a war on and life does not just go on the way we think it should. If he and the Thornton brothers run just the horses and don't invite half of Mississippi I don't see any objection. But mother this is not going to be some grand affair like he's used to. None of your coterie of old ladies with their suggestive comments about me marrying and giving you grandbabies to bounce. Both sides of this conflict would think we have supplies to spare and come take what they need."

"What about the sale. I think you should be there. Knowing your father, he would let'em wander through our home, picking and choosing even the house servants! Uncouth so-and-so's . . ."

"Mother, what has you so riled up? Did father do anything while I was away?"

"Yes Henry, yes he did; the most disgusting of things he could have ever done. Henry, I've been withholding information from you and

your father. You see son, what your father does not know is where
Flora began her life and how she's tied to me. His father did not buy her
for us, which is the lie he told, but she was passed to us from my father.
She was my father's half-sister. Flora is my blood aunt, so her tie to me
is heart tied, blood tied, and I love her. Your father, when his mind is
not cloudy with pride among his so called friends, and when he's not
showing off, loves her too. How could he not. I know son, I know all
about it. Even more than you. It's been the way of things from time
immemorial. I can't change it by wishing it was different.   But,
yesterday when they arrived the Thornton's asked if we had any house
servants to sale. For some reason, maybe under the influence of too
much whiskey your father called Flora in and told her to bring her boys
along. Well, she couldn't of course so she sent for several of the men
who are standing in for them. Immediately your father recognized the
difference but tried to cover it up by selling one of them to the brothers.
Later that night he went to her cottage and ordered her to call their
sons. When she wouldn't, couldn't, he beat her for disobeying him. No,
I mean he had her beat after a few slaps by him. Spurred on by over
drinking, he called the overseer and had her laid out, and shamed her by
having her beat. Henry, you've got to get my aunt away from here.
Your father is not the same man he was, and I think Flora is finally ready
to admit, even to herself that she must go."

"I understand mother, and it will be done. Where is Big Mama
now, in the infirmary?"

"Yes. Her body was cut up by the lash, and she's under with
laudanum. Please express my deepest condolences to her, son. I will
come after a while. Thank you love," she cried, wringing her hankie.

"Of course, mama. I'll go now," Henry began tearing up as he
talked to his mother and hurried out. First, he headed to the cottage to
find Tawnie. "I need you dearest. My father has lost what little mind he
had, and beat Big Mama."

Tawnie gasped, covered her mouth with her hand and grabbed the cape from the hook that she had just installed. "No! I'll follow you."

"I'd like you to nurse her, if you think you can stand to see what he's done to her. I haven't seen her yet, but I've seen what the lash can do."

"Of course. How awful. Is your father normally this aggressive to the women in his life?"

"I don't know. Probably, but my mother said he's getting worse while under the influence of strong drink. I'm going to apologize for him, and I'm sorry for what you are about to see," and they stepped into the infirmary for the enslaved.

"Nora, this is Miss Honey. Miss Honey, this is our mid-wife, doctor's assistant and nurse around here. Nora, Miss Honey will sit with Big Mama while you get some rest. How is she?" and he went and leaned over Flora, took her hand hanging from the bunk and slowly brought it to his lips and kissed it. He stared down at her chewed up back, and the heat of his anger consumed him.

"Alive," Nora sarcastically announced. "Fa now." Henry knew she was angry and approved of that anger. It was better than pretending she felt nothing, as most of the enslaved had to do.

"I'm sorry for what's been done, Nora. I wish I could take her pain away. I will leave you to show Miss Honey what to do, and Honey I got to go see my father. I'll be back shortly," and with those words he bowed to them both and walked out.

Henry found his father where his mother said he would, in his study. The room was built not square, but more octagonal, with eight sides. To Marcus this meant something, but Henry could never understand what. It didn't improve his disposition that's for sure, and definitely didn't make him more highly esteemed in Henry's eyes, but maybe in his own imaginings. He went to up to his father, who had just come from walking the Thornton brothers to their room to rest during the heat of midday. "Marcus, I won't even wait to have you deny it, just tell me what you thought you were doing to have Big Mama whipped by your bastard of an overseer? Tell me why, old man!" Henry leaned over his father and yelled in his face.

"You better back up boy. Who do ya think ya are raising yo voice in my presence?"

"I ask you that same question. Who do you think you are to lay a finger on my mother's kin? Do you know who that woman is? She's my mother's aunt, her father's sister old man! How dare you put your filthy hands and your filthy whip on her beautiful almost white skin! Is no relationship sacred to you? Your son's are expendable to ya, probably even me. And my mother, what have you done to her?" and he lifted his father from his desk chair and threw him back down in it, hard enough to hear it crack beneath him.

"Boy, if you ever lay your hands on me, I will strip you of everything . . ."

"You try it old man. You just try it and see what happens. So far, I've held my temper in check, but you don't want to mess with me, and you don't want to go down this road of who can piss farther. Believe me you don't. There's a war going on outside, but that's nothing compared to what you will see me let loose on you if you try anything. Ya hear?" and slammed his fist under his father's chin, sending him flying backwards over the chair, and onto the floor. He then walked up to the visitors suite of rooms, knocked on the door and when one of the Thornton's came to it, he told them that they had sold all this season's stock and that his father was indisposed. He asked them to leave as soon as possible, that yellow fever had broke out and was spreading on the land. He stood by with his pocket watch in his hands, and counted the minutes to see how quickly they would move out. He watched through the crack of the door while they threw their things together, and he had never seen men move so quickly. They set a record he knew, and were running out the front door all of three minutes from the time he looked at his watch. He wanted to laugh, if the circumstances weren't so sad.

He called several of his black bosses together and had a quiet talk with them. Two he sent to help gather his unconscious father up and put him in his room. He stationed them at his father's door, and gave orders that he was to stay in his room until further notice. The others he told to put armed patrols around the borders of the property, watch out for any strangers and keep anyone who did not belong, out. If anyone came around, they were to send word up to the house and get Henry's approval before they were escorted to the front gate. Henry or one of his trusted men would go and get them from the gate. No one was to get on the land without permission from Henry, not even his mother's friends or the attorney. Especially not the attorney.

After all this was arranged, he went back to check on Big Mama and Tawnie. He found all was well there and asked, "How are you doing?"

"I'm good, just a bit tired. How's everything at the house?"

"More stable now. I'm setting up safety procedures that I hadn't taken care of before. Your arrival woke me up to a few measures that I've been slack on. Thank you."

"I'm glad I could help. How's your mother taking all this?"

"I'm sure she's very unhappy, but known to be resilient, having lived with slaveholders for decades and in her own private hell for some time now."

"I'm so sorry. The world is messy. Well, as you can see Big Mama is resting peacefully. I don't want her addicted to the laudanum, so I mixed together something to replace it. It's from a plant grown here on the land called plantain, or ribwort. It has other names like pig's ear and band aid plant. Have the women aided by Nora pick the plant that has five parallel veins running the length of each leaf. They'll see that the leaf comes in several shapes and that's not the important thing; either broad or wide leaves, or narrow with lance thin leaves it's identified by its veins. Maybe I should just wait until Nora comes back in and tell her. You already think I talk too much," Tawnie told him, giving him her unconsciously seductive smile.

"Sweetheart, I'm sorry I ever said that, but I didn't mean it like you took it. Don't you know I wait in breathless expectation to hear your next words?"

"Hahahaha! "Tawnie laughed out loud, covering her mouth in surprise when she remembered Big Mama lay across the room. "Yea right. I bet you do. Small things to a giant, my love." she whispered.

"I know that's right, baby girl!" Henry said incorrigibly, smiling just as enticingly. "Are you ready to go? I could use a nap."

"Not yet. And napping is the furthest thing from your mind."

There went that smile of his again. He got up and kissed her lips, grabbing her bottom one between his teeth, nipping it. She giggled and pushed him away, and said, "You go nap, and I'll sit here and watch for Nora. I'll meet you at the cottage as soon as she arrives."

"I'm taking you to my place down in the oval tonight, so until you're ready I'm going to check and make sure everything is running smoothly and maybe go for a ride. Do you ride?"

"I do, and that sounds like a good idea. How about we have our dinner out there somewhere. I'll ask Nora to go up to the house . . ."

"No. I'll take care of everything. Just wait here for me, I'll be back later," and off he went. He thought over the way Tawnie had taken to delegating, even to him, and he knew that it was significant. He wondered if she was even aware of how she was becoming a part of him, a part of what he desired most, a place of peace that he could share with a lovable woman, one that could love him.

He made the rounds of the land, checking on the people, the horses and other animals, the crops including all the gardens, asking and answering questions, reassuring and being reassured that even though war was at the doorstep, all was well here on the plantation. They all prayed that somehow a miracle would happen and they would all be spared.

12 CHAPTER

While Tawnie waited for Nora to return from her rest, she wrote down description of plants that could be used for medicinal purposes. She wrote down and drew not only the plant needed but the mixing agents that should be available even here in 1863. She wrote that Nora would need to find apple cider vinegar, vodka, and pure olive oil but, if that was not found they could use animal fat such as lanolin, lard or belly fat from a baby goat or a lamb. She wrote that the roots could be avoided unless she was able to get them thoroughly cleaned. Set aside small glass jars to hold the mixtures in, and pour separate amounts of each mixing agent in individual jars, filling them half way. Nora could either send the children to find different kinds of weeds, or send out women who knew what they were looking for to pick them, but either way they would have to be separated and looked over for best use. Next to each description she drew a sketch, and wrote which mixer would work best. The list included *shepherds purse* a weed in the mustard family, *cleavers* a persistent weed that was rather sticky when touched, *chickweed* which she knew they would be familiar with since it was eaten as a green like salad, a common flower/weed the *daisy*, and of course the common *dandelion flower/weed* which the women were probably cooking too. She wrote down to look *for dock or yellow dock* which was appreciated by the native women of America for many useful purposes. *Groundsel and ragwort* are ancient hardy perennials that could kill livestock like tansy, and are not good for sheep, but have been known to be useful to humans. The entire *mallows* could be used for many reasons. *St. Joan's/St. John's wort* might be avoided by sheep but humans made wide use of it. *Self heal*, a scentless perennial mint is underappreciated by all, but could be valuable.

Tawnie wrote down all this from memory. Then she remembered that most of the enslaved weren't allowed to read, so she knew that her time here would probably need to be extended to help her darker sisters learn to read and write to get benefit from her herbal offerings. She prayed that her plan would have time to succeed.

While she waited, she made several large batches of the plantain to be used as healing poultices, and a large batch of it to be rubbed on as a soothing oil for friends and family on the land. She knew that eventually she might even need it for herself. The infirmary was well stocked so at some point the white doctor from town had evidently been around. Appreciation filled her for him, for the gift of his time.

She kept busy by cleaning the shelves of the infirmary, and while she was there several people came by for several different reasons; one had a simple splinter, another received a burn from the forge fires that she was ready to clean and dress with her newly made oil first and then the poultice.

Then, in walked a tall dark-skinned woman who was outwardly the most stunning woman Tawnie had seen since being here. Her skin had no wrinkles, no lines even in the neck, so she was still young. Her hair was braided in tiny corn-rows with beads or jewels of some sort intertwined and had no gray, but was a dusty brown. Her eyes were slanted upwards and were outlined with eyeliner, which Tawnie knew was not invented yet, so must have been applied using homemade materials, probably from burned coals. She stood straight and kept her head high as if she claimed status here on the plantation. Her dress was draped and tucked over her body, similar to a sari, like native people of India wore, but the colors were vibrant, the Kinte tribe's colors, and around her neck and wrists she wore strings of beads and bands of copper and brass. She must be from West Africa, with ties to the Gambian culture, Tawnie thought greeting her asking, "How may I help you?"

"Yo, gone back where ya come from. That's how ya can hep me. Who ya be any way? Where ya come from? Triflin heffa! Ya thank ya ken get in Massa Henry's bed, huh? Thar be no room fo three!"

"Well, if you don't need help with a medical issue, I suggest you leave," Tawnie told her, turning her back, dismissing the troublemaker.

"I belongs hea! Ya don't. Ya gets gone quick!" and then she turned and left.

Tawnie could hardly believe she actually heard the threats coming from the woman's mouth, threats unspoken but meaning quite clear. She knew it was true when she turned around and though the woman was gone, she could still smell the odor that had emanated from the woman's body. Not that it was a bad smell, just unusual; a mixture of cinnamon, cloves and dirty socks, musty, moldy, damp. What smelled like dirty socks. She didn't know how to describe it other than that, and didn't know of anything else that could smell like that, except maybe mold from certain mushrooms or other growths from the earth. She'd have to wait and ask Henry about the woman. Suddenly she felt uncomfortable, and wanted to be away from there. She went over to check on Big Mama, checked her back and grabbed clean towels to soak in the healing plantain oil. She removed the used poultice and replaced it with a fresh one. Even though she had the jitters and felt like pacing, she wanted something more constructive to do. She began washing the one window, wishing it had a screen and thought maybe she would tell Henry about modern ways to move air through close quarters like this infirmary. Fans were known of in this time, but none were used here. The concept shouldn't be that difficult to share. Then she had a light bulb moment, and sat down and wrote out a list of modern conveniences from her day that they might begin working on now, and bring to fulfillment. As she wrote, Henry returned with two horses.

Tawnie shared with him her concerns about the Kinte woman and he told her, "She's the laundress and works with cleaning supplies like lye is all," Henry told her looking at Big Mama.

"Though she was a nice looking woman, her disposition was as nasty as her smell. It hung around her and it was the scent of death. It was eerie."

"Some of the women here eat dirt, clay, starch and I don't know what else. Maybe she'd been eating dirt. I think I've come up with something. So that I can keep an eye on you, I'd feel more comfortable if you moved in with me."

"Into the big house?"

"No, my place in the oval behind the family gardens. I have room and would be grateful if you come," he softly persuaded.

She didn't need much persuading after having the Kinte woman practically threaten her. She knew what determined women were capable of, the methods they'd use to remove those they felt were in their way. Tawnie didn't want to leave herself open to be hurt so she quickly answered Henry to the affirmative, "Of course I'll come. I'd be lonesome without you now, too. Here's Nora. Let me talk to her for a few minutes so she'll know what's been done."

Henry moved over to try and get Flora to speak with him. Then he left off, remembering that time heals all wounds, and it had only been a few hours since it happened, last evening. "Big Mama, I love you, and I hope that gets through. Mama sent her love and said she'll be by shortly. I'm sorry for the fools we have to surround ourselves with. Marcus is in his room on lockdown. I took care of the overseer, driving him off the land. Rest now and get betta quick." She didn't move, but Henry really didn't expect her to, knowing she was still under the laudanum. He wanted to move her into a guest room of the big house, but didn't think Nora would want to nurse her there, more than likely running into Marcus which would not be a pleasant prospect for anyone. Marcus would have to be watched, have to be shadowed by the bodyguards that were now posted at his door. His unjustifiable attack on Flora was proof that his drinking was out of control and Henry remembered his paternal grandfather had a sad end because of it.

∞∞∞∞∞∞

Twenty years ago when Henry was a boy of ten, the Hazelton's had an anniversary party for the senior couple, James Earl and Lavinia called Livvy by everyone. Just about all of the land owners had been invited and all attended. The night was clear and bright, with the full moon shining from heaven on the happy party goers. The couple had been toasted, the meal had been eaten and the furniture moved for dancing. As the young people danced, the women sat chatting about babies born and marriages arranged, the men were out in and around the barn discussing things that the wealthy discuss, crops, sales and purchases, politics and who ran into whom at what cat house out in the country by the river. Suddenly one of the enslaved men burst through the barn doors and into several of the white visitors, spilling the drinks they carried over them. Looking to get into trouble, being under the influence of whiskey and other strong drink, they tried to grab the black man and take out whatever frustration they had on him; and having been disturbed they felt justified in doing whatever fantastical horror was brewing in their minds. The war gave them reasons for many acts they might normally not have carried out, nor participated in.

One of the men yelled, "How dare that nigga knock into me! What's he running from anyhow? Catch'em, right James Earl?"

James Earl was drunk and not thinking clearly either, so he said, "I'll get him!" and grabbed the reins of the nearest horse, jumped on its back and took off after the slave. Of course he went the wrong way, having not even seen the way the runner went. He galloped off; the horse had probably been rudely awakened and was unprepared for the rigorous ride and demands placed upon it. At the second fence, having cleared the low first one, a cloud passed between the moon and the earth, hiding the moon and the horse missed the fence altogether, slamming itself and rider headlong into it. James Earl flew over the horses head, landing on the hard ground. When they found him, his neck was at an angle, clearly broken. What began as a week full of jubilation, ended as one filled with mournful funeral preparations, because before the family could arrive from around the country, Livvy succumb to her grief and died.   Everyone forgot about the reason for James Earl getting on the horse in the first place, thank God. After that Henry was careful about what he drank and how much. Marcus wasn't.

Henry escorted Tawnie to the horses; a tame mare for her and a white stallion for him. He boosted her into the saddle, and then jumped on his own stallion, riding bareback. They had a basket full of food and drink, a blanket, and candles for lighting up the night in case they stayed out that late. The land was vast and Henry wanted to show her the whole plantation by horse, including the bodies of water, the cabins for all the families and workers, fields and buildings for storage. They road for an hour then walked awhile until he noticed Tawnie tiring, and they stopped. Henry spread the blanket out just as the sun was lowering against the horizon. They plopped down and set up the candles since it looked like they'd be out in the darkness. "Thank you for this, Henry. The sunset is glorious, and it feels good to be able to relax for awhile. How did you find everything and everyone?"

"The men are at peace with themselves. A few women had issues, and several heard, evidently from Nora or Sente about you."

"Can you tell me about Sente? Why she made the remark that there's no room for three in your bed?"

"Hahahaha!" Henry leaned back and roared in laughter. "Did she really say that?"

"Yes she really did! I'm happy you find it so amusing."

"What is that tone I'm hearing. Dare you claim to be jealous, my dear?"

"I don't claim any such thing! I'm just wondering what her position is in your life and around here, that's all."

"Well, her story begins when we were young. Livvy and James Earl traveled down to the Gulf of Louisiana for some long forgotten reason, and on their way back they attended a dinner and ball for Henry Clay the 'great statesman' at the St. Louis Hotel. Evidently they had a wonderful time, eating and drinking, being entertained by the French Opera orchestra. Before they left town, a message came that one of the women who worked in the laundry had a baby that she wanted someone to take before they made her dispose of it. Livvy, rather than see it put on the auction block at the crossroads, gave the manager fifty-dollars for her. The baby was female, Sente. She's been here ever sense. Raised right along with all the rest of us. To me she's like an aunt, so, to answer your unasked question, I have no interest in her in any way other than being a part of the family."

"That's fine. I can understand why she would want to know who and what I am, where I came from and how long I'm staying. The funny thing is, what would I tell her if she confronts me again? So, I need to stay away from her. Henry, another thing. I think I know why I'm here. I don't know if you've been staying informed on the political situation, but Lincoln freed all your people on January 01 of this year. He signed the paperwork in September last year, but because the Confederate armies won't stop fighting until they're all dead, it probably doesn't matter. And because of the war, there's no way the south is going to make any changes on their own, without being forced to, so the families might as well remain in bondage. If Marcus stepped up right now and said you can all go, with the war continuing where would they go, how would they go, and who would they go to? How would they eat Henry? I'm here to prepare my people for freedom. To help them understand that the roles they have now, can be the roles they have in freedom and can be very profitable. A cook can keep cooking, and feed the white folks, because who will do the cooking when the black cooks leave the plantations, Henry? Whoever shod the horses, will be expected to continue in that position. The women in the laundry house, who will you get to replace them? Has your mother ever washed a blanket, beat a rug, polished her silverware? Has she even cooked her own meals? The key to the plantations, harvesting of crops, who will do that once the enslaved walk away from here? You know what I would be doing, making plans to begin paying them. Take a census and find out who will want to stay and turn your dollars into gold. You've got to plan to keep these people on the land, and to do that you must pay them. Henry, evidently you didn't use your treasure to keep the people, but I suggest you get those jewels traded to somebody for gold coins! They won't be any good just sitting around, but they can be put to good use as payment to provide services that will be needed to keep this place solvent. Many of the current slaveholders and land owners will soon be destitute, they'll have Northern "carpet baggers", those land grabbers who will sweep in like garbage picking vultures and pay banks what the "southern gentlemen" couldn't pay because ineffectual pride will keep them from stretching out their lily-white hands to their black ex-slaves and working for the good of them both," Tawnie finally took a breath and stop talking. She looked at Henry who was looking back at her through the candlelight with not only an impressive look, but one of devoted desire.

"I hear ya precious, and you have my vote. Can we begin in the morning? Right now I have my own problem. Come here and let me show ya what it is," he said reaching for her. She went eagerly and they made passionate love under the stars through the rest of the night.

13 CHAPTER

The work began immediately to ready the people for the day that was coming. Soon, what President Lincoln had already done, would happen in reality. Millions of black people would be allowed to walk away from the only life that many of them knew. Most were born into slavery, but Tawnie knew that having been enslaved did not have to define who they would always be. Soon they would be free, and with that freedom would come great responsibility that she was sure they were not ready for. Adults would have the discretion over their own lives, their children's lives and for new life to come. Decisions would have to be made for future life choices, and because she knew what the outcome of history would be, it was on her shoulders to prepare them.

A school was established in the overseer's house and Henry went into town to get the duplicate equipment that the white schools were using. He passed word to the Quakers that a teacher was needed and would be well paid by the underground. That meant Henry would use treasures from the chest to recompense whoever answered his request. If what Tawnie said was true, they had about twenty months to teach, train, and equip everyone to move forward into freedom. Henry thought it would be to the benefit of them all if he could persuade them to stay here on the plantation. He would divide the land into plots, proportioning equal shares of four acres to two families to share. That way no one would be expected to work alone, but be given an opportunity to succeed immediately. The major operation of the land would continue, the new changes would be that it would be run as a little village like he'd heard were outside the cities of Great Britain. No more would only his family, the Caucasian side of the Hazelton clan reap the benefits of the black labor force. They would all have success because there was no other option. The war outside would not be allowed to creep inside and divide the family. The boundary for it would remain at the gate, and as there was now, there would remain sentinels posted to keep out those who would not and could not share the vision set for Ravenel House. Officially they were on lockdown!

"Everyone's raving about the school house. They send their appreciation, affection and promises to work extra hard just for you. A few said they will be the future doctors, lawyers, accountants, musicians, writers, preachers, and on and on. I encourage them to believe they can be anything their hearts desire. The women are setting up beauty salons to begin teaching each other how to take care of their hair, and even the white folks will be frequent visitors because right now they are getting their hair down by them. Several even asked Sente to teach them how to use the eye make-up that she wears. I don't know if they've gotten a response yet, but they are hopeful. They're also canning all the fruit, not wasting any as they've done before. Now they realize the profits that can be made by offering for a reasonable price any excess. Henry, I've walked around looking for a building to use as a store. I want to get your suggestion and approval," Tawnie stopped talking and raised her cat like eyes at Henry.

He'd been busy lately, and didn't have time to give her the attention that she deserved. He wanted to run away from all this, leave everything and take Tawnie, put her on the ship, and escape to the islands. But, how could he when she hadn't shown a shred of weakness since that first evening she gave way to tears. Not because she was afraid, but because she knew all the ways it could have gone for her. She could have ended up in the hands of a brutal rapist who threw her in the cotton fields, after taking her over and over that night. She could have seen the reality of life on some of the plantations around the south, the harsh conditions under which the black people labored, the uninterrupted beatings, the chains wrapped around human flesh to maintain control with humiliation and out of fear, and the constant flow of humans on and off the land due to buying, selling and trading of black flesh. He knew all the underpinnings that held this place and many like it together was done not out in the open light of day, but usually behind the pretty scene of the white mansion and expansive spread of the lawns filled with flowers of all varieties , and the magnolia and apple blossoms blowing softly in the breeze. Yes, he considered himself a gentleman, and yes he knew of a few here in the land of cotton and tobacco, but he also knew the others. The ones who had two faces; one that smiled gently, putting a person at ease in their presence, but who could in a blink turn the other face toward you with the gnashed-tobacco-stained teeth, whiskey fouled breath, snarling frown.

He never wanted her to see that side of life while she was here or anywhere else.

He took a moment to hold her, wanting to thank her for being there in this time of human degradation, standing up to life-altering events and making more from them than she had to work with. So he quietly said, "We're going to need a real doctor. One from the people who will be equal to the challenge of mending black flesh and not shy away from touching it. Whether or not what most doctors in town feel is real or pretense we need our own. We can't count on them to come now anyway with the land on shut-down and confederates dropping daily, over- extending the few there were. I need you to talk with Nora and find out who would make a good candidate to send to medical school in the north. We're going to have to take a trip. This trip is going to be dangerous for several reasons. One, we may start out on water, but eventually we'll have to cross through the lines on land, passing through south and north combatants. Two, we'll be traveling with more people, those not use to role-playing and being devious. Three, the time it will take to be away from here. I don't have that many trusted men who are used to leading, giving orders. The system is set up for them to take orders not give them, to be subjugated, not to gently ask or persuade others to act. I need my half-brothers and maybe Christopher Jefferson. My God Tawnie, we have to go back to the Caribbean and get them! That's the only way."

"I see. You're right. Unless you put the ones here through extensive training. You will have to choose between limiting the time in harvesting and using them to train and prepare them. Also weapons training. You're going to need more in order to arm them. Pitchforks and machetes won't equal to a loaded gun. We're going to have to turn the forge into an armament factory, one that puts out weapons of war instead of implements of farming. Even swords can be used close up, so they'll have to learn to make those too. Can you see how that could work instead of risking a trip to the Caribbean now?"

Henry rubbed his thumb across his chin, and then down the side of her face, contemplating her words and trying to see the vision she put in his mind. "Your right. I have to think bigger than I've ever done. I have to see beyond today and try to see what you see, what you know about the future and that is almost impossible. The rhetoric that has spread here was that all that was needed to whip the north was a few months, and look now. It's been several years, many battles and more to come for several more years. I've got to think in terms of winning each daily battle around here and not what the south will eventually do, because our objective is not the same. Our goals in fact conflict. We have much work to do. I'll go choose a few men who I think will work as leads, and you go talk to Nora. By the way, I saw Big Mama up on her feet today. Do you know she harbors no ill will toward father? She said the drink caused the harm to her and not him. Can you believe that?"

"Henry, she knew your father as a young man. She knew the real Marcus, the virtuous man, the sober man; the one who was before he became poisoned by chemicals put in drink to alter the mind and destroy the bodies interior like a blood-sucking leech, and will eventually if left unchecked eat away at the exterior too. She has unwittingly come to care for him, whether that was her intention or not. We have to remember that. Emotions have no time limits, they continue in a person long after the other person changes and becomes someone else. It will take time for her heart to catch up with what her eyes see and her mind knows. Henry, is there any way to detox, or cleanse your father of the drink and from today forward keep him from drinking? And soon he will have to come to terms with the harmful effects of smoking too?"

Henry again had to try and wrap his mind around the new ideas that would become the norm of tomorrow, but was as yet foreign ideas for today, here in this year 1863, almost 1864.

"I see almost like I have x-ray vision, your mind churning through the new information you're taking in and turning over. I'm glad that you're a reasonable man, an open-minded man, because Henry if I could show you even a tiny glimpse of the future, it would blow the top off your head right off! It has to be accepted in tiny doses, like laudanum, but you don't have the luxury of tiny steps, we have got to be ready so that we win, so that my people, our people now that you have claimed a side by accepting me, win, and are more than what we see them as now. Many will not be able to cope with the changes Henry, and will end up in asylums filled with the insane. Oh, yes, that too. That and worse," Tawnie enlightened him quietly. "And while you come to grips with the truth, mull over this. Women won the vote, fought for equality and wear the pants in a lot of families. Now I'm no feminist, I like my god-given role just fine. But in this fight, I am all in, and I want you to see me as an equal in every place but the bedroom. Okay? There, you will always rule, always dominate, can always be on top and I'm more than happy to let you, sweetheart," she stated matter-of-factly while batting those cat like eyes of hers. Then she purposely switched her rear end seductively and walked away, leaving Henry with an open mouth, stiff and hard everywhere else.

14 CHAPTER

He went to gather his leaders. A few, those on patrol and those keeping an eye on Marcus were capable, would be willing to take on even more responsibility. He mentally reviewed others who might be ready physically, mentally and even spiritually. The physical could be built upon; weight added by building up muscle, strengthening the muscle already there and toning up flesh, though not through hard work, because all of his people worked from dust to dawn. But by focusing the training on certain parts of the body. The mental would not be as easy to spot; sometimes the abnormal, those with an unusual and unnatural taste for blood, those who were warped from birth or became unbalanced by their environment could hide what they were. And often times there were so many, like the soldiers who eagerly volunteered to go slaughter their brethren. Then the ones who stood out were the normal; they were the ones called freaks, the ones who were persecuted. And lastly he had to determine who was fit spiritually, who would sicken with each casualty of this horrid affair, who in fact had a conscience. Which men would stand firm to doing right, even though the majority went down one path, the path of wrong, the popular path? Who would steer clear of that path and take the least traveled path, the right path? Those were the ones he wanted. Those men would have his back!

"Joseph, Oman, Seven, Eric, Philemon, Herman; I know this is going to sound like you're dreaming, but it's not a dream. I need your help. The war is not going to end like everyone thinks, not going to end as soon as everyone thinks, and the south is going to lose. The reason the south is going to lose, is because the south is wrong. The leaders are delusional and they are, frankly, crazy. Lincoln signed paperwork last September that stated on January 1 of this year you would all be free if, and here he made two stipulations; those states like this one, who chose to break away from the United States and form a separate country of southern states, who believed in trading in black flesh, stayed out of the Union, you all would be free. He also stated that if the North wins this war, you would be free. That means, because the Confederates are remaining apart from the nation as a whole, you are all free. But, if you step outside these gates and told a white man you are free, what do you think he would do? Do you think he would say congratulations, I am glad for you?"

"Naw! They prolly snatch us up and hang us, or shoot us or some other bad thang, Massa Henry," Oman said with intensity.

"That is very true Oman. The President also said that any man who does not stop fighting is breaking the law. That anyone who bothered a freed person of color, would be held accountable to the law. Do you think that if you were to go to the sheriff and tell him about a southerner who hurt you, the sheriff would help you out and go after the white man?"

"No way, Massa Henry! He'd take the side of the white man," Joseph spoke up.

"Every single time, Joseph. Men, friends, because from now on you have to begin thinking of yourselves as my equal, I know this is hard to understand, hard to remember, but I also know you are all up to the challenge, of doing so; I am no longer your master. My father is not your master, and my mother is not your mistress. I am Henry, or Mr. Hazelton, father is Mr. Hazelton and mother is Mrs. Hazelton. As you have also probably heard, father is not well. He has allowed the drink to take over his life, and the choices he's been making lately are proof of that. He is being guarded, and he is not to be without a guard. As the south continues to decline, their feelings for you, not you personally but the group of you, will deteriorate. If you think they hate you today, wait until they continue to lose battles. And in the end, they will see it was all for nothing and their feelings will rage. The laws today are being broken, so what do you think will happen when they lose the war? We can't even begin to comprehend the evil deeds they will plot against you. It will all be with the Devil in the lead, because there is no other who could produce evil but that one. Most of them will never believe what is happening, when the end of it comes. They will have the backing of most religious leaders who at this moment are not only complicit, but who are leaders, praying over them. The north will come in here like a hurricane with all the vigor, all the capability of their factories, and with the backing of a better educated, trained and armed military, and we will have to be ready. Right now, the south wonders why I, an able-bodied white man is not out fighting for the cause, and as more of them fall, they will demand that I fight, and that I bring you all along to fight too. What will you do Seven, Eric, and you Herman?"

"Stop them at the gate? We's gon have to make sure there's guards all round the place," Seven shared.

"What we gon use to do that, Henry? We gots machetes and some knives, but what if they orders us at gunpoint?" questioned Herman in his broken English.

"You are exactly right Herman," Henry said pointing. "That's why I called you all together. We need to get more guns, and gun powder. We can easily make more machetes and swords, and we'll have to learn how to use them. Training is what it's going to take, drills just like the soldiers go through, and I'll need all your help. We will each divide the men up into groups of seven, those first groups will train and they will be the generals, the leaders of all the following groups. Each time we ready one team, the leaders will gather seven more and train them, and so on and so on until every man is trained and has a position in this army. From now on, that's what you all are, soldiers in Hazelton's army. I know what the Bible and the Koran state about killing. They also state that a man who does not provide and protect his family from danger, is no kind of man. We are not taking up arms to battle for some kind of Ideal or for pride. This battle will be about our very lives, to protect ourselves and our families. That is the difference from the other soldier's. They fight because those in power have used propaganda on them, brain-washed them into believing a falsehood. The powerful are greedy, they fight to keep hold of their way of life, their puffed up ridiculous sense of pride. And because it was written several thousand years ago, "pride cometh before a fall", we know they will fail. Now, we have to train, then our first trial will be to raid the armory downtown. Keep this quiet, because father has his spies, those who despite everything he has done, will remain faithful to him, regardless of what they personally believe. They won't be able to break free from that old mentality of master and slave, bowing and scraping. It's not all the fault of the freed man, it's going to take time to move some people beyond the today into tomorrow, but move them we must. To accomplish that, we will need to use all the stealth we have, because we can't let them out to spread what's happening around here. If any of you know one who would turn traitor to our cause, it will be up to you to watch that one, and if necessary silence them. Can you do it?"

"I can do it!" Oman spoke up, standing.

"I would has to do it, whether I wants to or not," said Herman.

"It won't be easy I knows, but, the other choice is to sit down and die nah. I could do it," Joseph answered.

"I's could an would do it," stated Seven. "In fact, I knows of one of'em who would just as quick thrust a blade in any of our hearts. That one there!" and Seven stood up and pointed at Philemon.

At that, Philemon jumped up and tried to run, but Seven had anticipated his move and was on him, tripping him as he ran past, jumped on his back like a grizzly on a salmon, wrapped his massive beam-like arms around Philemon's neck and with one twist, they all heard it snap. Philemon got up, shook himself like a wet dog because of what he'd done, feeling the effects of having killed another man. They all took a moment to adjust, to take in how quick it all happened right before their eyes. Just what Henry had been saying. It wasn't conjecture anymore, it was reality. And it stared them all in the face.

"Seven, what do you know about this man. His running proves that he was a traitor for someone. Was he the spy for Marcus?" Henry asked.

"One that I know about. I'm sho there's mo," Seven said quietly.

"Go ahead, if you can, and tell us. We're listening," Henry and the others sat back down.

"Big Mama told me there's a snake in the grass round here. So, we been on the watch. I's member mo than once seein Philemon slip out past me in the cabin at night, and head towards the big house. I knows it wat'nt good goin on in the dark, so I followed mo than once and saw him and Mr. Hazelton talkin, and Mr. Hazelton was pointin toward the cabins. Next I knew, several members from families went missin. I thinks Philemon was helpin Mr. Hazelton make sales behind yo back and pocketin profits hisself. If we goes and looks in his belongins I bets we find his share of the sales."

"Eric, would you take Herman and search Philemon's side of the cabin from top to bottom, under boards and inside the fireplace. When a man would take profits from selling his own people, he would not want those profits easily found. Tear his side up if you have to, and thank you. We'll see you both out at the orchard. I want to check on the border there," Henry told the men, and he led the others with him. "I think we should train out here in the orchard. That way we're not clearly seen, we can use the trees as the enemy, and as some place to duck from each other when we train with one group as the enemy," he said looking for any disagreements. They all agreed and went with him to scout the area, clearing any obstructions. "We begin training at six in the morning. By eleven, we'll break until the cool of the evening, because we should probably include night training in our schedule right away; I'm sure the enemy won't only come in the day. At eleven until one we will rest. Beginning at one until five, we will work the land, making sure we get the lots divided, new cabins built, a store found, and assignments divided for the next weeks. At five we go to dinner and rest until seven. At seven we will all meet back here to go through some evening and night training. We'll train until the first man complains of being tired, probably around ten. That should make for a full day. Our bodies won't have any other choice but to strengthen and harden itself for battle. Any questions, ideas or comments? More heads are better than one?"

"Henry, I'm thinkin only two or three groups should train at any one time. The others should begin makin weapons, and enforcin the fencin round the land. Is there some way to add some kind of spikes to the tops? I don't think the way they are now will stop anybody from liftin each other over the top. I remember slippin off with several of the women as a younger man, over the tops of those fences," Joseph admitted.

"We better go have a look," Henry acknowledged, thinking that Joseph might be on to something.

When they got to one fence, Oman said, "We wouldn't wants others to think we trying to build the place into a fortress, but that's zactly what we gon do, so we want to make spikes that don't look like spikes, just decoration added, right?"

"Yes, Oman, you're right. Seven, what do you see?" Henry asked, wanting everyone of his leaders to be equally involved.

"Well, Henry, like Oman said, the spikes should not call attention to the fact that they are meant to keep people out, but if they are placed in a way that a person could not help but have to come in contact with them we could make a few, and the design would have to be such that they themselves are weapons. Each one would have to be razor sharp, and spiked," Seven answered, looking over the fence with an eye for detail.

"Joseph, once you helped the women over to the other side of the fence, was it easy to get to the ground?" Henry asked, trying to picture Joseph falling on the other side. "The height is such that you'd have to catch her after dropping down risking an injury to your foot or leg, it seems to me."

"Yeah, that's why we did it only a few times. I wonders if we put razor sharp areas along the fence at mid-line where a person might try to first grab hold? And once they tried it once and got cut, they'd not try it the second time. And, one way to use fewer men posted around here as guards would be to dig a shallow trench along here where we's standing, and put spikes inside and cover them up with decorated grasses, or ground cover of some kind."

" I can picture that. Razor sharp strips connected on some kind of line. I'll check into that at the mercantile shop in town. Eric and Herman are coming, let's go see what they found."

Henry led the men to meet Eric and Herman, and Eric extending his hands spoke, "Well, it looks Seven was on to something. Hidden under the boards under the bunk was a pouch of coins. Looks like he been paid," and he dropped the pouch into Henry's hands. Henry shook the coins out into his hands and counted thirty one silver coins

"How ironic. One more piece of silver more than Judas was paid for turning over our Lord Jesus Christ to the Romans. He was a traitor too you know? I guess this is a lesson for us all. Let's head on home, and bury Philemon before someone notices him. I'll do it with Joseph and Herman, the rest of you get some rest, it's been a rough day. See ya in the morning at six sharp. Good evening to ya," and walked toward where Philemon was left, and the others went on their way.

15 CHAPTER

Over the next weeks everyone worked harder and were prouder of their individual accomplishments than any other time that they could remember. The digging of the trenches about equaled the cultivating of the fields, but there they were able to use mules to pull the plow, and the trenches were too close to the fence to do anything but use the human back. Because the people knew who they were doing the work for they found pleasure in it. They labored not for others to profit from their misery, but for their own safety. This attitude moved them to do the best work they'd ever done, and stay at their labors longer they ever had without complaint. One day while Henry was training in the orchards, Eric ran up to him and said, "There's a Quaker man at the front gate. He say he has passengers," and walked back to show Henry. When they got there, and Eric saw he wasn't needed he went to take the place of Henry in the orchards so that the training proceeded even though one leader was absent.

"Welcome Mr. Still. Come, we have much to discuss," Henry shook the gentlemen's hand and led him through the gates. Henry led the man to the orchards where he showed him what they were up to. He could trust this man, this Quaker who was a leader and influential conductor on the underground. So far, between the two men they had helped six hundred humans escape the bonds of slavery. Mr. Still might bring those who needed help getting out of the boundary of the US to Henry, and those who could be moved closer to the north Mr. Still handled. Henry thought over the help the Quakers as a whole were giving to the cause. He had spoken to a lot of the leaders of the sect who encouraged the Still family to work with Henry as much as possible, as he was known to the underground to be the most prolific of the conductors among families. Mr. and Mrs. Still were often invited to dinner with Regina and Henry outside of Ravenel House as Marcus did not appreciate the teachings of the religious sect. They were major players in the abolition movement against slavery here in the US and overseas in the United Kingdom. They began espousing the

Underground movement in 1688, near Philadelphia, Henry was told. Many of them became known in this century for trying to do more than just speaking about its horrors but actually getting involved and opening their homes as stations on the railroad. In these homes families would be fed, bathed, clothed, and shown compassion. They often needed medical care, child care and even midwifery. Mrs. Still told Henry and Regina that she counted nine babies that she had delivered, alone. Not all Quakers began and kept to the condemnation of slavery, but many of them owned their fellow man. It took a century to stop some of them from involving themselves in the "peculiar institution". As more and more of them progressed in their knowledge of the Bible and began practicing what they preached, they realized it was an abomination to make another work for you, work in the place of your children while they went off to have their lives enriched through college, travel and recreation. Labor in your place while you sat back in your comfortable lethargy and paid them nothing. Wrong to dominate another person, especially when you knew that the ones being dominated had lives, cultures, futures and plans for themselves in their mother lands.

The Quakers eventually took the lead in getting slavery abolished, having the freedom to speak, publish, congregate, and preach against it, whereas the black man was limited in what he could do, being under the gun himself. The tireless work they did was not forgotten and their efforts were hailed by many ex-slaves as being directly from the "hand of the Creator". Because of them, other groups got on board and began rallying against slavery, and that's how Henry and Regina became involved. When Henry was a young boy, the Quakers invited several artist who had works depicting the cruelty of the government sponsored system to their church and Regina took Henry. One artist who accepted the invitation and attended was J.M.W. Turner. He brought his oil on canvas depiction of the slave ship Zong, whose captain ordered 133 members of its slave cargo to be thrown overboard into the shark infested waters, so that the insurance could be collected by the insurers. This was the catalyst that moved Regina.

Another Sunday they were invited to hear a visiting speaker preach a sermon entitled, <u>What Would Jesus Do About Slavery?</u> and that talk, using Holy Scriptures as its bases, was never forgotten by either one of them. Their entire congregation began taking an active part in whatever small way they could through fundraising, sewing, knitting and crocheting projects and sharing what they knew of the evils of slavery wherever they went, and soon word spread. It took every last effort by all colors of men to finally get it abolished, and many died for their trouble.

After touring the training grounds, Henry led him to the shop where some of the blacksmiths were making the needed barbed wires that Tawnie sketched for them from memory. These would go into the trenches as they had discussed after the hidden razor edges were completed at mid-line points along the fence. The principle issue was to keep the enemy from going beyond that first grab of the fence. After that they wouldn't want to go any further, which was absolutely the point.

Mr. Still was amazed at the transformation the Ravenel House plantation had undergone. He asked many questions and Henry answered each one. He most wanted to know about the future and what was to come immediately after the war. He made an appointment for a later visit so that he could return and discuss more with Tawnie. He had come for a reason, to ask Henry to get a woman and her children to the north, but now there was no need to have them leave. He asked Henry if there would be room to move the family here, since their way of life had changed and the woman and her children would be free. Henry told Still that she would of course be welcomed. A return visit, with the family in tow was to be made soon.

Mr. Still stayed long enough to have a shared meal with Regina, Henry's mother and Regina invited Big Mama to sit with them because Marcus was still having his meals in his room. Regina spent half the day with him so after the initial days of detoxifying, he calmed down and now had a better disposition than even a week earlier. He still had not called for Big Mama to ask for her to forgive him, but no one was holding onto their anger over it, knowing the madness that can overcome a person who abuses drink. Henry invited Tawnie to dine with them and she was introduced as a northern free woman who returned to help her family and got swept up in the war and now had to stay. Most of that was true, it just wasn't mentioned she time traveled to get there.

After the meal, Henry and Tawnie walked Mr. Still to the gate and he told them, "The woman is Ms. McClendon. She is coming with two children, a four year old son and a two year old daughter. What I could get out of her was that she was raised in the big house, her mother was the cook and was also keeping the master's bed warm after his wife died. Things were fine until he found himself another wife, and that brought all kinds of negative consequences to their happy home. Well, the master ended up dead and the new wife ran off, so Ms. McClendon's mother was accused of murder and is now waiting to be hung, because you know the system is not going to give her even the pretense of a trial. If I had a friend bold enough, I would ask if he thought it might be possible to get her out, and out of the country. I doubt that there is a man in this business who could handle such a dangerous mission. I imagine all any of us can do is pray that the truth prevails and that Lillian is given her freedom. Well, I will see you at the appointed time and day, and thanks so much for your hospitality," and he bowed to them both and was gone.

"Hmmm, if that didn't sound like a challenge, I don't know what would, do you?" Tawnie asked Henry teasingly.

"I don't," he said solemnly.

"Well, I guess I will finally see the real Enrique` Salvatore, in all his glory and full gear, eh, senor?" and she winked at him showing a smug smile.

"Maybe. I'll have to find him and ask. Right now I am exhausted, so let's go home." He pulled Tawnie into his arms and they watched the night sky as bats swept through heading out to feed. Tawnie felt saddened at the sight because she remembered the exact scene in her other life with her other family on a night like this. She let the feeling flow through her and move on, not wanting to bring forth tears which would do no good. Like Henry, she had a job to do, and having been chosen she would fulfill her duty to both families.

∞∞∞∞∞

At the appointed time, a few days later Mr. and Mrs. Still returned with the McClendon's. They accepted lunch with Regina and Big Mama while Henry and Tawnie extended hospitality and the use of the weaving house to Ms. McClendon and her children. Tawnie prepared their first meal in Henry's cottage, and they dined their together with her serving. She was a wonderful cook and incorporated plantation dishes with modern ones. She prepared greens and smoked neck bones, cornbread dressing, sweet potatoes and for dessert she baked a peach cobbler. Every drop was eaten, and afterwards they all went for a walk to tour the quarters where the McClendon's would spend the majority of their time.

While the little ones were introduced to several other children their age and went to play nearby, Ms. McClendon, whose name was Shayla shared her story. Her mother Lillian was a mix of Scots-Irish from her father McClendon and a Seminole woman, Pearl. McClendon came from Ireland and bought land in Mississippi from a Frenchman. Somehow he met Lillian's mother during a period of transition for the Seminole, possibly during one of the wars between her people and the government. Shayla didn't have the full story but one helped the other and they came together. Lillian was born several years into their relationship and grew up a most beloved child. Pearl and McClendon would have welcomed more children but none came so each poured their shared loved into Lillian. She took after her father and was a porcelain complexioned beauty with green eyes. Her hair was straight and hung down her back in light brown tangles because she was always putting beads and feathers in it that never stayed. Several of McClendon's associates wanted to marry her, but no one knew the proper etiquette for marrying a mixed race woman of native descent, so Lillian chose her own men. Before she could settle down with the love of her life, a black enslaved carpenter that worked weekends for her father, her father lost his money and sold Lillian to a banker. She found out that her father's love was conditional. The condition was whether or not his own livelihood was affected. Lillian worked in the home of the banker and his wife, until the wife died. He moved Lillian into his bed, and the next year she had Shayla, but what he didn't know was that Lillian continued seeing the black carpenter secretly and Shayla was his child. The banker evidently had a drop of black blood too, because when Shayla was born he did not balk, but accepted her as his very own. Shayla, like her mother was a gorgeous child and grew to be even more beautiful. She has Hazel eyes, not quite green and not quite golden brown but a mixture of the two, her lashes are long and brush the tops of her cheeks, her hair is a mixture of light browns with highlights of gold that run throughout , and that hangs down to the top of her hips. It falls in waves, and draws men in. Lillian took great pains to see that Shayla knew her father, Lance Brooks the carpenter and she arranged at great risk to herself to see that they spent time together. Lance truly loved his daughter and wished he was free to do more for her. But Lillian and Shayla never complained and took what time they could with Lance. As Shayla grew and reached puberty, the banker began exhibiting an unusual passion for her. Evidently he did know she wasn't his child, because when she reached seventeen he raped her. She became pregnant and Lillian delivered her son, Jacques. When she turned nineteen he raped her again and Lillian delivered her daughter, Puponne. Lance, when he heard what the banker was doing to his precious girl, made plans and when the banker married a white woman, Lance visited them on their wedding night, gut and castrate him and all right in front of her. She fainted, and when she came to she packed and took off afraid Lance would come after her. Before they could get things cleaned up, the Sheriff was locking Lillian up.

"Since mother nor father told Sheriff who actually did the killing, Sheriff locked mother up. Father got away, got word to Mr. Still and here we are. Now Mr. Still will try and get mother out, and move them both, father and mother out of the country. I want to thank you Mr. Hazelton for taking us in," Shayla ended her brief account of her life up to this point. She sat with her hands clenched around a handkerchief and both Henry and Tawnie went and sat on each side of her. Tawnie pulled Shayla into her side and held her, trying to share some of her strength with her through osmosis. They all sat quietly together, each reviewing what they had just heard. The contrast of what they were seeing in nature on this beautiful day, and what they had just heard of Shayla's life was astoundingly different, and took a moment for them to digest. They understood that life was hard, even tragic since all would eventually end up in the common grave, buried six feet under, but hearing how ugly and messy it was for her and her little ones was indeed heartbreaking. Henry felt justified in asking God to forgive him for what he was about to do.

16 CHAPTER

Enrique` Salvatore stepped from the dark, away from tree line that bordered one side of the the building that held the Sheriff's office. H e listened with the ear of a moth hiding from a blood sucking bat, and when he heard several rats scampering through boxes next door, he knew it was clear. He beckoned to his men to spread out to the areas discussed. He stepped up to the door of the office and walked inside. Looking around, he saw a man asleep at the desk. He moved up to his right side and stuck a blade to his temple, saying with a deep voiced-Spanish accent, "Senor, I can drive this into your brain before you exhale, so don't. Where's the Sheriff, por favor?"

The deputy wet himself. He wasn't a full-time deputy so he wasn't use to having knives pointed into his skull and wasn't about to die for the Sheriff. "He went to dinner and never returned. I'd say he's down at the Red Door, fornicating."

"Si. You have a choice, and I suggest you take it. Give me the keys to the cells, and quietly walk out of here and go home. Comprende?"

"Like you said, one choice. I'm taking it," and handed over the keys, stood up and left.

Enrique` walked through the office and down the halls toward the cells. At the end of the row, he found a woman curled up on the low bunk. He called out to her, "Lillian, I've come to take you away to the land of freedom. Are you ready for that?"

Lillian sat up, not in fear, as she had made peace with whatever came, knowing that she was innocent. "I am," she answered quietly. She didn't know if the presence before her was saint or sinner, but she knew that what he offered she was ready to accept. She stood and walked to the bars and Enrique` unlocked them. He held out his hand to her, and she placed hers into it.

"Come, I have your daughter and grandchildren ready to visit with you before we get you and Mr. Brooks out of the country. Is that your wish?"

"It is, thank you," she whispered.

"Then let's do this," Enrique` answered.

Just as he arrived, he departed, with the stealth of a hunter. When they got outside, he gave a whistle, and moved back into the trees. His men surrounded the pair and they moved quietly through the forest to horses that were waiting. Since there were probably confederate soldiers nearby, they didn't gallop away, but walked the horses without making any noise down to the water. When they reached it, Lance Brooks stepped up, took Lillian into his arms and kissed her deeply. That's when she had a moment of weakness, and gave way to tears. The others gave them just a moment, then they led the way onto the ship.

The ship did what the men did not allow the horses to do, take off like the wind. They sailed straight to the islands without mishap and made it there two days short of the last trip. Everyone was able to relax and they celebrated the day before landing with music, dancing and cutting up. Joy was the word of the trip, and everyone was full of it. Enrique` put away his persona and Henry returned. Tawnie was thrilled that Enrique` did not have to harm anyone. She knew that not all endings would be as peaceful.

Tawnie wanted to encourage Henry to get to know Shayla and her children better, so at every opportunity she pushed her forward toward him, and made her own feet take steps back. It was hard to give him up, but she knew Shayla would be the one to walk with Henry into his future. She was a beautifully strong woman, who would make a worthy companion for him. Her children were healthy, intelligent and loving, good examples for others and a sample of the children that she could give to Henry when Tawnie was gone. Tawnie knew that she was not an angel, not totally self-less, so it would take time to break totally free from him herself, as long as she has to stay here. So until that time came she was his.

She knew that she was a moral person, but in this immoral world that she now inhabited, she would have to blend in. She would have to hang her morals on a hook at the door, just like she hung her hat. Here, as she bide her time, she would to behave as the rest.

"Shayla, you are now free. What do you want to do with your future?"

"I never thought about anything for me, but I do want my children to have everything they need. A good education, work that they enjoy and the good things in life. I want my daughter to be able to choose the man she wants, and even I will have no say in that. And, I want them to be able to choose for themselves whether they want children or not. I would hope that they can live in peace and quiet with no threat of war. The only thing I want for myself is to be able to watch them grow up and make their own wise choices," Shayla admitted. "What about you; do you have children?"

"Yes, I have two children. They're in the north where I live. I'm here helping Henry prepare families for the freedom they now have, but can't take advantage of until after the war. My father's family is related to his family, we share the same blood."

"What do you think of that? Sharing blood with while folks?" Shayla asked her.

"Well, considering we're all related through Noah's sons, I don't see how any of us have much choice. Family is who you share your life with, who you love and who loves you. Do you think you could love a white man if he is kind, loves the children and wants to share his life with you?" Tawnie asked her.

"I'm not sure. Every white man I've known has been deceptive, traitorous pigs. Haven't you found that to be true?"

"To be honest, there is bad in all men. Look at what Cain did to his brother Abel. Since then, we've seen nothing but how men choose to use the free will that they were gifted with. I think the scales are tipped toward the negative use of free will, but as long as we still have choice, as long as even a few use theirs for good, I see hope. Two men in particular have been good to me, have loved me and I've love them. They have shown much courageous, compassion, devotion to me and others despite great upheaval in our environment. Have you never had that from a man?"

"I've had a form of love from my father Lance, but he was stifled, inhibited by distance, bondage, and so was limited in what he could do."

"I know that now, with freedom for him and all of us, he will be able to do more, show more and express his love to you and the children, and even your mother in the way that he has always wanted to. The reason I bring this up, is because at some point I will have to return home. I want to know that when I leave, Henry will have someone, a beautiful, trusting, devoted woman just like you to love him. It's too soon I know, just getting out of one situation to expect you to be ready for another, but please, think about it and your future. I know Henry would be good to you. Now, to change the subject, what type of work did you do in your mother' house?"

"Mother and I did most of the lighter chores, but we have several women who helped with the heavier work. I know *how* to do the work, she and I just didn't always *have* to. I know how to cook, and I love to bake. I make all the pastries, cakes, cookies and such. I wonder what the differences in my life will be with freedom? You have been free awhile now, right? How does it feel to be able to say no to someone?"

"I will show you. You and I will role-play. I am someone who you don't want to touch you. Now, remember, you can start out politely saying no. And if the person doesn't listen and obey, you step it up a notch, by saying no louder and putting up your hands to ward off their advance. And then, if they continue to press you, go all out and use your hands or whatever it takes to get them to understand that your no means no. Ok? Let's begin. I will come up to you, and remember, you can say no."

The two ladies practiced for an hour until Shayla could say no and mean it. She started out not being able to tell Tawnie no, but Tawnie continued until she tested her by going too far and Shayla came at her with fingernails bared like an eagle's talons, and aimed for her face, but Tawnie blocked her and grabbed her, twisting her around, and then Tawnie knew Shayla was ready. Tawnie talked her down, back to calm and the game stopped.

"Thank you Tawnie. You've helped me prepare myself and now if someone wants to act like the banker, I know how to protect myself. I will have to show my children how to do so, also. I have an idea! While the men practice their skills, you and I can help the women with theirs."

"That's a wonderful idea, Shayla. We will gather the women and divide them just like the men. We will work together and teach them self-defense training. Shayla, you will be able to add teacher to your resume`!"

"Resume`?"

"Yes, your list of accomplishments is called resume`."

"Oh, Tawnie, there is so much to learn. Will I be able to do it?"

"Of course! Half the battle is fought. As women we work harder, but in the end we shall win!"

While they sailed to and then from the Caribbean, having said their goodbyes for now to Lillian and Lance, they reviewed and practiced what they'd gone over before, and made plans to do more upon returning to Ravenel House land.

17 CHAPTER

And so the women began their training. They were divided up into groups and the other jobs were continued as well. Cooking had to go on, the schoolchildren had to be taught, the sewing to repair the clothing of all the people had to be done. And they learned how to prepare for anything. Tawnie had a group that she led first, and since she knew more she taught the women not only assault training, but weapons training as well. They worked with the new blades that Tawnie designed, because the weight of the ones the men used was ungainly. One of the women saw the barbed wire and came up with a design that uses little metal balls that she trained the women to fling in slingshots. On another day, someone designed a bow and arrow that fit comfortably on the backs of all genders. Tawnie realized that the gunpowder that was stored in barrels around the place, could be used to make Molotov cocktails that could be tossed at the enemy, just as well as the cannon explosives that they might use on them. So she came up with a casing that held the powder, blasting cap and fuse. Then she realized what she had made was an actual bomb. That shook her for several days, but thrilled the men, who set up a celebration at the end of that week.

Using the techniques of the bomb making, the men made fireworks and set up a bar, the women set up a buffet and helped the children arrange a place for games and they partied all night, on Saturday. After the children went down for the night, the musicians set up and the adults danced and sang a new song that Tawnie wrote. She told the group, "This song is what I call the blues, and is dedicated to all of you, my dear new friends."

'Not everyone can be a friend

to equal the friendships that they've been shown

Because not all of us have had friends

so friendships to us are unknown.

Next time you have someone say

let's be friends to match all friendships others have tried

Then we can be the friend to at least one other

and prove those who said we can never be friends, have lied!'

Everyone learned the song and sang it the rest of the night.

The next day those friendships were tested in the worse way. Marcus got away from his guards and tried to round up his spies, but because everyone knew they were now free, the old ways were not going to work anymore. They surrounded him and the spies, and marched them back into the big house. After locking Marcus back into his room, they led the other two to the front gates, told them to run and shot off guns over their heads. They squealed and took off running down the road. Since they didn't want to be a part of the new order, they could stay a part of the old and get out.

No one knew if they led the rebels back to the plantation themselves, but they next day a contingent of them showed up at the gates and demanded entrance. One group moved the children into the big house with Regina and Big Mama, and Henry came to the front and told them the only way they were getting onto his property was with an invitation, and they didn't have one. Several soldiers from the back line moved up and grab the fence to climb over; that lasted all of one second. They drew back their hands and found them shredded by razor sharp hidden seams in the fence. They ran back to the back line hollering, spraying blood everywhere and the next row moved up. This group pulled their sabers out and tried to slash through the openings of the fence. The women on the plantation took out their slingshots and slung the metal balls, hitting them in the head, and chest. This group fell dead. The last group pulled their guns and tried to fill them with powder and shot, but before they could they were blasted sky high by cocktail bombs. When the smoke cleared, a clean-up crew stepped up, dragged the bodies inside on to the land and burned them. Nothing was to remain from the rebels, but everything was burned with them. No proof that they were ever at the gates, was to be found, if anyone did come around asking. After everything was cleaned and rearranged as it was, everyone went back to training. Now they knew what could happen, that the rebels, the confederate army might at any time show up and demand entry. They were prepared for anything.

Tawnie talked to some of the women that night, letting them know what a good job they did, that everything went exactly as planned and as they had trained for.

One complaint from the women was that the clothing they were given by the Hazelton's were hampering movement. Tawnie knew exactly how to remedy the problem, and showed them how to sew a seam in the skirts to make them into pantaloons. They worked so well that the women decided that they would make a pattern and design some for children also. Then after the war ended, they would sell them to the public. Tawnie was so excited, because each enterprise that started while she was here, she had faith that it would continue and when she returned to her time, she could trust that her people would be set up for the future.

One day one of the young boys found Tawnie and asked her if she would ask if he could preach. She told Henry about him, so Henry asked the men if they would bring their families to the grove, in the open area on Sunday. Everyone attended, even Regina and Big Mama. Benches were made and set up in a half-circle. Lil John, the child who asked to preach and share the word did just that. He stepped up to the center spot and had the crowd entranced with his little voice raised and lower at different points like the octaves on a piano. He said so many 'can I get an Amen's' that Tawnie thought she was in the Baptist church back home. There were two types of people in the world Tawnie knew; one type were the son's of Adam, those of the flesh who sought out only the things of the flesh, and the other type were those who were touched by the hand of God, the one who sought higher things, spiritual things, and Lil John was one of the latter. After he preached he sang, and that too was like the angels. The people joined in and then the musicians pulled out there stringed instruments, their drums, their mouth organs, and the littlest even brought spoons to bang together, and it sounded like the best music in the world. It went on all night. The people seemed to be the happiest that Tawnie had ever seen them, and she knew why. Living life without guidance from the spirit was not living at all. Praying was just an open dialogue with the Creator, and she thought, we all need that.

∞∞∞∞∞∞

Tawnie had been so inspired from Sunday, several days later she took time out to write a new poem, the beginnings of a song . . .

The sun is shining, a new day is dawning

So stop yo frowning and thank the Lord.

Our new dignity is shining, so brightly it's blinding,

The train is coming let's get on board!

We'll all stand together, not one day, forever

See the conductor coming, he's opened the doors.

A sign that he's smiling, all his teeth are a gleaming

The hard work continues, let's get on board!

Henry told her she was a poet, and that he was extremely proud of her. To show her how proud, he invited Shayla to cook for them in his cottage, and told her to bring the children

. He wouldn't allow Tawnie to lift a finger in preparation, but let Shayla do all the work. After they ate, and Shayla cleaned up they heard music coming from the grove and knew that the musicians would be celebrating life all night. Henry pulled Tawnie into his arms, and she showed him steps of dances that she knew. He held her mostly, and whispered words of love into her ears. " Girl, I never knew I wasn't living until you showed up. I feel so complete with you, and I never want that feeling to end. I didn't know you were satisfied with me until I saw you hang up your dress and put those pants on, then I knew who you really were. You're simply beautiful girl, and I love you. I know, you might disappear at any moment, but I wanted you to know how I felt. Since I first saw you, I've been wanting to tell you that you are the kind of woman that makes a man, any man want to live forever. Live and do for you, to wake up to see your smile, to not want to sleep because he would have to stop looking at you. Darlin, to tell you the truth I might just have to destroy those pearls just to keep you here. What would you say to that?"

"Henry, you have made me happy too. I doubt that it would matter what you tried to do to them, it probably wouldn't work. We each have a path to follow, and I know I am here for only awhile. You've got to come to grips with that my love, otherwise you won't be able to live the kind of life you're meant for after I'm gone. I found out being here what living is all about, and you made that happen because of your love for me. I will always have that no matter where I go, no matter who I'm with. When you are with Shayla, you will remember me with kindness, and that would make me happy. Thank you for that. You are a good man Henry, the best of men."

Tawnie stepped out of his arms and pulled Shayla up from her chair, and placed her in his arms. Henry then danced with Shayla, holding her as he had held Tawnie, and Tawnie knew he would be able to move toward Shayla when she was gone. Tawnie gave them time for a couple twirls around the room, and then moved to hold them both in her arms and the three of them moved in a slow dance. The children giggled to see their mother happy and relaxed. Henry drew them up from their chairs and brought them into the dance with the adults. He

113

stood them up on his feet and danced them around, and they giggled even more. It was a wonderful night for the little family. After the adults put the children down, they sat up discussing the progress around the land and what changes they'd noticed. The streets were mapped out, the store was built and almost filled. Everyone was working at jobs of their choice. A church was planned near the grove, but not to take the place of the enjoyment derived from activities already held there. Everyone agreed that there was a time for everything under the sun. Traditions remembered from the homelands of the people could continue with Henry's blessing. He had his traditions, so who was he to deny anyone else theirs; to each his own he always said.

18 CHAPTER

Of course life has a way of kicking up dust and making a fuss whether you are doing everything right or not. Weeks went by with no trouble from the outside. Then there came trouble from within. One man wanted to test another man and they started out just bickering. After that did no good, the one went after the other with a knife. The women of the men screamed and went running to Henry's cottage to get him to come help. Tawnie was there, and so she went. She had that way about her, and went right up to them with boldness and said, "Well gentlemen, today is just as good as tomorrow to die. Whoever is the winner of your dispute, will have the pleasure of being handed over to the Sheriff. We have just begun to enjoy the freedom that some are outside these gates dying for. The majority of them would like to see you dead and buried, so why would we want to quicken their pleasure by killing ourselves? Men, we don't need to give'em help. Here on Ravenel House land we use what we have to fight the enemy outside, not our own within. Now, we don't have a police department here on the inside, we didn't think it would ever be necessary. But I would ask you two to choose several men and talk to the carpenters and arrange to build a jail. And guess who our first residents might be?"

"So sorry ma'am. Sorry Junebug," and Theo walked away.

"Junebug, is it finished? Do one of you have to be thrown out of the best thing you've had in order to get you to see that life without this place is true hell? I've seen the decimation of the black community because the men and fathers put themselves and their pleasures before their women and children. They allowed petty disputes, male pissing contest to overrule their good sense and destroyed each other. The alcohol, drugs, loose women, competitive incompetence, and outside influences were just an excuse. What was really behind the battles was the inability to be men, real men. They never knew how, because they didn't have examples of men to raise them. Why? Look in the mirror. They killed each other? That's the easy way. Let's try the hard way, to get along. Then maybe our children won't end up being raised by only the mama's. Maybe they won't end up packed in crowded tenements in overcrowded cities, competing with the roaches and rats for food. Maybe the circle of recidivism in prisons can be broken. We need to give our black babies a chance to live. Do you hear me, Junebug? The next black man who tries to kill his brother, will be banished!"

Henry missed it, because he was in the orchard training with the men. When he heard about it, he couldn't stop laughing. His little lady had confronted two of the largest men on the place, and she had bared her teeth like a bull dog and they'd backed down. He was more than proud. The only question he had was why weren't the men too tired to get into arguments. Why weren't they so tired from building, training and family life that they didn't fall into bed every night like he did?

"We've got to increase the training schedules to all day for some men, and then the next day they're to spend all day working in the fields, preparing the land for planting. They must have too much time on their hands!" he barked out the next day to the leaders. And the leaders listened. The little streets became like graveyards, and the houses like tombstones, because the families were in by dusk they were so worn out. After three months of the grueling schedule, the men begged to return to the former schedule, promising to police themselves and make sure the trouble makers received their due. Henry agreed.

Never again, that Tawnie knew about, did the men fight to the degree that they had. The threat of banishment was felt by all, and no one wanted it.

While the men went through their adjustment period, the women grew closer. They had too much work to do every day and they needed each other to get through it. The sisterly bond grew and they shared together like never before. The children thrived under the care of the variety of motherly personalities. Tawnie told them it took a village to grow a successful town of young people. The mothers took what she said seriously, believed that she knew what she spoke, and trusted that if they did not take good care of them they might all end up in the slums. The women promised themselves not to allow anything to distract them or take away the progress they'd worked hard to achieve. They tried to laugh everyday because Regina told them that humor was an indication of intelligence. She did have the sayings.

She and Big Mama shared in the care of the children, and that was one of the reasons they thrived. Big Mama told them to always give special consideration to their elders, to care for them and show them respect. Age did not matter, family was made up of many ages. The two women had never allowed anything, especially a man to come between them. They were related by blood and understood that they needed one another to get through the trials of life. "Flora, have you received any messages from the islands lately? How is everyone?" Regina asked her aunt.

"Everyone is fine, Regina. Simon's wife Rosa is with child. The school is progressing, all due to the supplies delivered by Henry during his last trip. Gabriel found a woman and they want us to try and make it next year for the wedding. They all send love, of course."

"Wouldn't that be wonderful if we can get away soon for a sail to visit them all? Marcus is getting better with the lockup and detox, so maybe he will be able to sail with us. Would you like that, too?"

"I got no say in that," Flora told her niece. Yes, they had shared a man, but as an ex-slave, Flora did not have a say in who came into her bed. Now that slavery had ended, it would be awhile until she too learned to say no.

∞∞∞∞∞∞

Flora never thought about anything beyond the present day and getting through it. All her life she had to take orders from others, and put them before herself; she couldn't even care for her children in the way she would have liked to. But now, things were different. Tawnie was teaching her what's what; teaching her the new world order and at last she would soon be able to choose the kind of man she'd always wanted. A tall dark and handsome man. A man like the leader Joseph. He was her age, and she wasn't a mare put out to pasture yet. She suspected that Joseph had never married because he might have an affection for her. She hoped so. Soon she would leave here and go be with her sons in the Caribbean. She would have to get a backbone and ask Joseph to go with her. She thought over her past and the encounters she'd shared with Marcus. He was a big man, and he'd brought her some pleasure sexually, but he was her master and she was his slave, and she could never forget that. He'd tried to take everything from her, and she knew it wasn't because she wanted to give it to someone. He'd never even asked her what she wanted. At times, when he wasn't under the influence of the drink, he tried to be the man that he knew he should be, was raised to be. But something in him, some issue that she was never able to get him to admit to, held him back from being a truly lovable man. The kind of man that she saw in Joseph. Over the years they'd shared a few encounters, he'd been up to the front door and they spoke. She's wanted to grab hold of him even then, but she was trapped, trapped in her situation. Now she was free of any encumbrances. She could do anything she wanted to do.

Joseph was at that moment thinking of Flora. She was correct in her assumption that he was single and had not chosen to marry because of her. Over the years he had watched and waited and now his chance at happiness had come. He found her exotic and luscious. During training all he could think about was her, even thinking he could still smell her scent in the air from the last time he had come across her. He wanted her, and planned on asking her to go away with him, if not marry him. His heart ached when Marcus had her beat; with deadly ferocity he wanted to crush him and the overseer under his big feet, but the time had not come. He was nothing though, if not a patient man. His time would come, and Marcus would feel his wrath. Marcus was due an ass whooping and he was the man to give him one.

After training one evening, he went down to the water and jumped in. He bathed, shaved and doused himself with a mixture of scents made up by their own perfumery here. He walked for a while thinking of an appropriate gift for his one and only future.

He picked flowers, cut some beans, grabbed some ears of corn and a piece of white lace that was given to him by Enrique` Salvatore after a mission one night several years ago. He'd been saving it for her to wear on their wedding day, the day they became one and put them into a basket to take as a gift. He ached to see if she was healed up. He'd never felt for a woman the way he felt for her. He walked up and knocked at the back door, where he knew Flora went in often times when leaving the cook house. She was nearby and pulled the door open, saying, "Joseph, my goodness. It's good to see ya."

"Flora, it's so good to you too, see ya doin well. Do ya have time to come and sit a spell, I'd like to talk wit ya?" Joseph enquired of her, slipping in and out of the slang used around the plantation. Sometimes the endings were dropped and sometimes they weren't depending on nervousness, time, who's being spoken to and self-awareness.

"More time now than ever befo. Come, let's sit under the lilac's, it's nice and sweet there."

" Flora, I've watched and waited, loved ya from afar, plannin and hopin that our time would come, and it has, it is now. Would you come away wit me, and be my woman. We can jump the broom, or stand befo Henry as our Captain of the sea and marry. Don't matta none to me, whatever ya say."

"Yes Joseph. I've felt the same way. I can start living for myself now. I can come as I please and do as I please. Choose the lover that I know will make me happy. I know you've wanted to be that lover and I'm proud that you still want me after all this time. My son's want me to come live near them, be a grandparent to my grandchildren and that's what I want. If those plans fit into how you see the rest of your life, then yes, you can have me and gladly."

Henry moved closer to her, took both her hands in his, brought them to his lips and kissed each in turn. "Flora, starting from today, from this point on my love is here to stay. I'll never try to bring ya down, to bring ya nothing but joy and happiness. You're now mine, and the standin up part is just fa show. I've longed for this day, worked for it, bowed and scraped for it, cause I knew our day would come. You saying yes, has made me the happiest of men. Thank ya my love. Whenever yo ready, I'm ready. Can ya come be wit me tonight down in my cabin? In fact, move in when ya ready."

"How bout, come Sunday we meet in the grove and have Henry marry us. We can stand up befo God and men, and jump the broom. How's that sound?"

"O' Lord, thank you!" he said looking up to heavens. "And thank you Flora." He pulled her into his arms, and kissed her deeply. They sat that way for awhile, contemplating the future.

19 CHAPTER

That night, Flora did slip down to the new Hazeltown, and eased through the door of Joseph's cabin. He was wide awake, naked on the bed, hoping she would come. "Joseph, are ya still awake?" she called out in a whisper.

"I am, come. Welcome. Follow the candlelight," he told her from a separate room in the back. While some of the carpenters were happy with the room they had in their cabins before they were free, others built more rooms onto the cabins they used, and still others moved altogether and started from scratch, building complete new homes for their families. Henry deeded the plots of land to the family and had each deed registered at the courthouse. He had the right to do so because Marcus had turned over the land to Henry during one of his more lucid moments.

"I had a change of heart, and decided why wait. Who cares really if I'm with the man I love now or later. Time don't stand still, and me or you ain't getting no younger," Flora stated, feeling a little nervous. She saw his arms extended to her and moved to him. He lay prone on the bed. She noticed the size of the bed, that it was long and thick just like her new man, the headboard which was made out of limbs from a white birch tree and had carvings of nature cut into the wood. She could pick out butterflies, dolphins leaping, crabs, and much more. "Is this the standard bed around here?" she asked in awe, sitting on the edge.

"No. I used the old bed for firewood several weeks ago. This bed we just finished and moved in yesterday. It's for us Flora. I began the design when freedom came. I will take the headboard with us when we go, but the frame can be given to whoever wants the cabin. Can you pick out the two crowns? Those are for the royalty that will lay under it, forever more."

"I love it," Flora said, standing up and first unwrapping her hair. It was wrapped in a colorful chignon, and when unwrapped he could see that it had been braided and then coiled around her head. She let down the coil first and then took it out of the braid. It was a blend of colors, but he could see that it had some grey sprinkled throughout its intermingled strands. When she finished unbraiding it, it stretched down to her lap and she shook it out. She leaned over Joseph and it spread out around him, covering his face and shoulders. He pulled his hands though it saying, "Who knew all this loveliness was hidden under that cloth. If it was up to me I would outlaw covering the hair of the women. Let everyone see the charm of all hair. No one chooses what they get, having no say in curly or straight and there is allure in all women. But you, woman though art splendor itself." He ran his long fingers along her shoulders, across the tops of her breasts and down the middle to her core, and across her navel. He worked them back up to her breasts and circled her areola's, taking time with each one. Tweaking each nipple, he pulled on them pressing until he saw a reaction in her face. Behind her eyes, her sparking eyes the color of a wild stormy sky he could see many things; hope, desire, lust for him, even fear. Maybe she feared that he would not appreciate her gifts. He knew what she offered and knew that Marcus would not have returned to her night after night to beget six sons on her if she could not keep him feeling some kind of pleasure. Joseph tried to push those thoughts aside, realizing that those days were over; it was his time now. He slipped her camisole all the down to her waist, and while she untied and unbuttoned herself out of her clothing he feasted. Wherever his fingers went his lips followed, igniting her senses and Flora moaned in pleasure. He could feel her pulse quicken at her throat as he licked there, slowly inhaling her essence. She moved her body closer, until he slid toward the middle, taking her with him. Now completely naked, he turned her so that she lay on her back and he leaned over her. He took her all in, still not sure how he had been successful at getting her to say yes. He wasn't sure that she knew his worth yet, although he always knew and never doubted himself. He would show her his value and now that she was really here, he would start with giving her the best night of lovemaking that he was sure she had ever known.

Flora rubbed her hands along his shoulders, mimicking the paths he had make on her skin. Then she leaned up to taste his mouth, running her tongue over his lips first, then encouraged him to open to her by licking at each corner. He took the hint and opened to her, and they teased at each other's tongue, then sought the sweetness inside. He wrapped her into his arms, releasing her after hearing her begin a deep throated moan. With one arm under her, he used his other hand to seek the treasure at the apex between her thighs. Once he found it, he slowly explored it, teasing and tapping, greeting and welcoming. She opened and closed in excitement. He worked her to a fevered frenzy, and found her ready, pulled at his length, lubricating his swollen head with a homemade oil and then found the valley of her being and plundered it. He aimed and plunged, aimed and plunged, withdrawing after each successful hit inside her wonderfully slick core. They each went to work to bring the other along for the ride to the top of the waterfall and back down, screeching and soaring all the way to the bottom. Flora gasped and locked her knees around his middle, never wanting to let him go. He understood the feeling and told her, "That's just the first round, my love. Take ya time, rest and I'll go get some water." With that she let him go. All night they gave love, accepted love, shared love and made each other feel so rapturous that tears fell from their eyes.

∞∞∞∞∞

Flora never realized how wonderful good love could be. Before dawn, she slipped back to the Big House and her room. The next morning she found Henry and asked if he would perform her wedding on Sunday. He hugged her to his broad chest and said, "Congratulations, Big Mama. Who is he?"

"Joseph de la Croix. He's my choice Henry. As soon as we can, without risk of harm to anyone, we'd like to travel to the Caribbean with you. I don't have much but Joseph has a headboard for our bed we'd like to take along, please."

"Whatever you say, Big Mama. It's done. Do you have everything you need for the wedding? Why not have all the ladies in for an afternoon tea party so they can help you celebrate and give you a few things for your new home. I'll get you anything you need, just let me know. Do we have all the foods and drinks you would need?"

"If we have a party, yes we are well stocked, thanks to you. You have made life so much easier for us all my dear. Don't make me start crying. I'd better go check on Marcus. Love you."

"Love you more," and he slipped out the back door and back to the training grounds. Henry wondered what kind of trouble he faced before the end of the war. It was almost time for confederates to surrender and he would be glad when it was all behind them. The only thing he feared was that Tawnie would disappear from his life before he could come to grips with the possibility of her lost. But that would have to wait. He had too much to do.

Saturday, before the wedding of Flora and Joseph, Regina sent word around that all the women were invited to the Big House for a tea and lunch. All the ladies crowded into the rooms on the first floor. Everything was set out and ready, so no one would have to spend time away from the guest. Each lady brought a little gift for Flora and Joseph. Regina kept a list so Flora could thank them each one. A few items received were a little basket of individually wrapped teas, a set of embroidered napkins, a matching table cloth, curtains for her soon to be new kitchen windows, and a gorgeous white bed spread with hand stitched lace edges. Evidently the spread came from Regina, and she had several of the lace makers add several rows around the edges. Flora pulled out her dress for the wedding in the morning, and everyone said it would be nice to gift Joseph with a shirt and pant set that matched. So several of the ladies ran out to the sewing house to get some matching cotton material. While the dishes were being washed, a few of the ladies were getting the materials and supplies for the wedding outfit, and a few others were helping Flora into her gown for a last fitting. There was no problems with the dress, so they whipped up the shirt and pants for Joseph, and then someone had the idea of whipping up several of the same design but different colors for Henry and the best man, and the groomsman. So the ladies got to work and were at the Big House when Union soldiers came knocking at the front gate. Regina accompanied by Tawnie went down, hoping that when they heard her northern accent they would move on, or at least not burn or loot the place. "Welcome gentlemen. Come on in, we ladies were just preparing for a wedding, but the least we can do is feed you."

The soldiers came in and spread out around the front porch. The ladies rushed around gathering up the leftovers that they'd just put away. They grabbed a platter and piled sandwiches, sweet turnovers, apples and peaches, pieces of fried chicken and deviled eggs and carried it out. There was a pitcher of lemon-aid whipped up, and Tawnie poured whiskey in it, hoping to get the soldiers if not drunk, tipsy so they can put them out. She did not want the men to get into a major fight, it would only lead to the Union soldiers being killed. At this point, the plantation men were too well prepared to allow themselves to be defeated by a few soldiers, be they north or south and the way that was best was to get them out of there before all the men noticed.

"Lieutenant Colonel Drake, ma'am," the handsome one in charge said to Regina, bowing. He was about six feet two, and about thirty-five years old. He had a thick handle-bar mustache that move when he spoke. "We've just lost a skirmish to the rebels down near Elkins' Ford. I'm wounded, and would kindly appreciate the assistant of a doctor or at the least a nurse if one's available. My men could use a day of peace, quiet, and a little rest, ma'am. Would you have men folk around that I need to confer with?"

"Colonel Drake, I am Regina Hazelton and this is my assistant Tawnie Hazelton. We are happy to provide a nurse for your care, and your men can camp on the lawn; we will try and see that they are comfortable. Here's the ladies with provisions, a meal for tonight and a bottle of my husband finest whiskey. Sit, please. May I join you in toasting the Union?"

"Thank you ma'am. To the Union." The Colonel sat, used his good hand to toast, drank from his glass and promptly fainted. Good thing he remained in his chair, because he was a large man.

When the Colonel woke up, he was settled in his tent in a cot that had a fresh mattress, a plump pillow, was being looked after by Nora. Nora had removed his dirty dressing and was cleaning the wound.

The Colonel looked into her eyes and asked," Where did you learn to clean and dress wounds so well ma'am?"

"I'm nobody's ma'am, just call me Nora, Sir."

"Thank you Nora. Did they allow you to go to school?"

"Sort of. When Ol'Massa's sista graduated school, he allowed her to come down here and teach me. Somebody had to care for us, them, birth babies and do what needed doing like this. No white doctor is available to come way out here on a moments notice," Nora told him.

"Well, I for one am indeed grateful that they did. My regiment lost its doctor awhile back, and I'm not sure any of those that's with me now could have done as fine a job as you've done."

Nora curtsied and left the tent. Regina went in behind her and with her chair in hand, seated herself by his bunk. "How are you Colonel? I wanted to let you know that you didn't embarrass yourself. You stayed in your chair, and just dropped your head. We all knew what had happened rather quickly, lost of blood. I've seen it before. We have a lot of births around here and the women often faint. You look much better, your color has returned. I brought that bottle out to you, and we can finish our toast. I want you to keep it for yourself, my husband has given up drinking. Not by choice, mind you. How is the war progressing Colonel? Does this loss for you mean the north is losing?"

"No ma'am. Not by any means. We lost because we got turned

around, didn't know the terrain, and walked right into a trap. These damn rebels are giving all they got, but it won't be enough. They don't have the manpower, the military strategy, the equipment, the weapons factories, nor do they have right on their side. The north will win and that's a fact ma'am."

" I want to be honest with you Colonel. My husband is a southerner through and through, but my son and I are abolitionist. We are a station on the Underground Railroad and our people have been freed. As soon as word reached us that Lincoln had freed them, we complied. Most of them had been freed, we just made it official. Where are you from Colonel?"

"Born and raised in Illinois, ma'am. You have a beautiful home here. Thank you for your honesty. Are all the men off fighting?"

"They would be if it was up to my husband, but it wasn't. Because he over drinks, he had to take the treatment, and right now he's locked in his room, under guard. My son, Henry had the sense to take control of the estate several years ago. My husband allowed it, and so Henry and I run things. Do you need anything Colonel before we all turn in, we have a wedding tomorrow. You rest and heal, and we hope you're not disturbed. Oh, Colonel, we have guards around the land, twenty-four hours a day the gates are secured. Don't you worry about the rebels, my son has all that under control. I'll send in your sergeant now. Good-night Colonel, and sleep well."

"Good-night to you ma'am, and thank you for your hospitality."

20 CHAPTER

On Sunday afternoon, Flora was given in marriage to Joseph by her great nephew, Henry. He also acted as priest and married them. Flora was naturally beautiful, her gown just made her more so. She carried an arrangement picked by the little ones that she helped care for. Several of them walked in front of her and behind her, throwing petals and seeds, symbolizing that life flowed in a circular motion and marriages were meant to continue that circle, because usually babies were soon to follow.

Her dress was ecru, and the ladies had made Joseph an outfit in the same color. Regina and even Marcus attended and stood nearby. The male attendants were all wearing the same shirt as Joseph, but in different colors, gifts from the women. The women were dressed up but they didn't want to overshadow Flora, so they wore styles of their own. Flora wore her hair down, and all the women kept the old ways of head coverings off. Everyone played their roles and it went off without a hitch There was an abundance of food, so Joseph encouraged the soldiers to participate in the banquet.

"How is the war progressing Sergeant? Can you get a sense of the morale of the men?"

"Well sir, all I know is the north is better supplied. We may lose a few battles, but the war will be won by us. The south's thinking is all wrong. To hold people against their will is called kidnapping where I come from. I thought the laws of the country were the same. But, to have a few people try and establish a set of barbaric laws is just not the way of civilization, not the way that any human should think. As far as I know all the men in this troop feel that way. They really want to do right by the enslaved and help them get their freedom that Lincoln instituted almost two years ago. Some of my men wanted me to ask if that's the way you all feel? You whites, that is, and pardon me sir if I step over my boundaries here. We just want to know?"

"Yes, son it is. We all feel that way. Can you tell by how we live that there is something different about us?"

"Yes sir. We've been commenting about it and we are sure happy we got here and not on one of those hate-filled reb plantations. Do you think the north will win sir?"

"I know they will win. It's just a matter of time. Are the all the men well; was it just the Colonel who was injured?"

"The others we buried, sir. I have a question for you, if I may. Would it be possible for me to return here and help you after the war, sir? I know you will need professional people, artisans and craftsmen."

"What skill or training do you have?"

"I am a teacher sir. I have a brother here and a friend who might also like to return. My brother works as a carpenter, but not an ordinary one; he makes musical instruments, violins, viola's and all manner of wonderful pieces of art. He's highly skilled after spending four years in Vienna. Our friend is also an artist; a painter. He uses oils, chalk, watercolors, whatever he can get his hands on. Oh, and the pieces he produces. You will be amazed when you see them."

"When the war is over, please return and you will be welcomed. We will have many to teach and train, to prepare them to either remain here, or move on. But no one will leave without an education, training and a livable skill. None will leave without money to set them up, all the Hazelton's will have something and be someone. Others will come, when they hear what we will accomplish, and the work will go on for years to come. Come back and help us."

"Thank you sir. May I say it has been a pleasure meeting you all here on the land. I will spread the word when I return to the north that there are some southerners who are still human, some who still have love and fellow feeling, compassion and mercy. And sir, may God bless you all."

"Thank you my friend. We will see you soon. Vaya con dios, go with God," and Henry shook his hand, bowed to him and left.

Henry went to find Tawnie. He fixed himself a plate, and went up to the big house. He saw her from afar standing on the porch, sunlight twinkling and shimmering off of her body. She was wearing a gold dress with puff sleeves, that just touched her ankles and square neckline that dipped low to show off the tops of her petal soft breasts. If he looked hard enough, which he caught himself doing, he could just make out the rusty colored areolas that surrounded her grape-sized nipples. Her hair, usually braided in one fat braid slung over her shoulder, was loose and flowing radiantly down her back, softened further with a halo of daisy and rose petals. She made such a picture that he wished the artist were here now to paint her. He needed to have something of hers to keep and cherish always, whether she stayed with him or not. So he ran back to the Sergeant and asked if the painter friend was in the group now. He was, and the friend was found, brought to Henry, supplies found to capture Tawnie as she was on this day on canvas.

The finished painting was a masterpiece. At the end of the day Henry toasted the painter and Tawnie with a bottle of champagne. Tawnie could see herself but not as she usually was. Here was a more delicate Tawnie, a more womanly, riper Tawnie, as if she were with child. Then she claspsed her hand over her mouth, thinking, oh no, it can't be true. Then she tried to remember the last time she had bled. She couldn't remember. What she did know was that she had lain with Henry just about every night since she first arrived. She put her hand on her lower abdomen where her baby bump would soon be. She was carrying Henry's child she knew.

Tawnie did not think she should tell Henry yet, if at all. If she remained here over the next seven months that's one thing. If she, over the next few weeks returned to 1983 she wouldn't. Why worry him. She'd wait and see, before she decided. Maybe he would guess. That night, after everyone was down for the night, she discussed children with Henry, and if he wanted any. "Dahlin, girl, of course I want my own children. If I am blessed to have them, I would be forever grateful, as grateful as I am to have known you. Do you realize that it's almost 1965. In just a few months, the war will be over and life as we have never known, can begin."

"Henry, knowing human nature you can guess how long it will last. Hasn't it been about every fifty years that a war starts? At least you'd be too old to fight."

"Let's talk of something more pleasant, like your portrait. I will have it rolled up and put in the attic on my eightieth birthday. You can find it there if you do go back. The silver, the gold, all the family heirlooms I will store in the attic. Inside the silver teapot, I will leave you a message as to where the other pieces will be, just in case the place is looted. You found the treasure chest, so you should be financially stable for the rest of your life, and your children's lives. If I leave behind children, they will have our last name of course for the males, but the females will hyphenate their last names, always putting Hazelton first. You said your father is a Hazelton, so his great-grandparents came from here. Now that you know who your people are, maybe you can set up a foundation in our name and take care of the family. I think it would be nice to gather down here once a year, reunion or family party. I will leave a journal or letters at least every few months. As I get older, with less to do, I'll probably be glad to sit on the front porch and write in a journal. Somehow, I will let you know what went on around here. If you go, that is. Frankly, I think you will be here forever."

"We know that wishing aint gettin."

"Let's go to bed. I'm depressed now."

"Henry, what do you think of Shayla? Is she the type of woman you'd go for, if I wasn't here? Could you ever love her if I go back?"

"I can't think of another woman with you in my arms, Tawnie.

Right now all I want to do is concentrate on burying myself deep inside you. If your mind is on something else, stop and redirect, okay?"

"Hahaha. You make me laugh."

"I'll give you something to laugh about. Where is your tickle spot? Your feet," and he began tickling her feet. "Your under arms," and he tickled her there. "Your belly," and he pulled her gown up over her belly, and saw what she didn't want him to see. When he saw how rounded she was, he gasped. "Well well well, what have we here? Is this the reason for all the questions about children?"

"I didn't want you to know yet. It looks like we're going to have a baby. Henry, if I go back, and I've had the baby, would you want me to leave it here with you?"

"Yes, I would only hope that it's old enough to be off the breasts, but young enough not to have known that it's mother would never see it again. That would be too sad. I don't think both of us should have to have a longing for you. It will be bad enough for me."

"That's the bad thing about this situation. I think there are wonderful aspects, and then some not so wonderful," Tawnie admitted. "Well, what do you want, a boy or girl?"

"Right now, I just want you. Let's get back to where we were."

"Your were tickling me; there?"

"No, before that. Here," and he pulled her over his throbbing manhood.

Tawnie noticed that their lovemaking that night was different than other nights; though still a deeply satisfying, thrilling ride, Henry was gentler with her, he sought out her pleasure more than usual. Always the gentleman, he was the epitome of what that word really expressed. He was a man who not only took, but gave first, bringing his body in control to give her the ultimate release.

Over the next few weeks, the Union army was encouraged to participate in the training that the men continued to do. The Colonel was back on his feet and began taking part in the daily workouts. When he could see that his regiment was even stronger than the day each one enlisted, he was ready to return to engage in another battle, and hopefully bring this war to its rightful conclusion, victory for the Union. On the day they prepared to depart, Regina and Flora, Joseph and Henry walked the Colonel around the land and showed him all they had been accomplishing. He was impressed and when they reached the front where they had begun he said, "Now this is what I see America looking like very soon. Somehow we have got to come together as fellow humans, one nation seeking guidance from our Creator on how to direct our steps. As Lincoln said, 'a house divided . . .' and he was taking the words that had been written over a thousand years ago. So it should have been no mystery what was going to happen even ten years ago. I think my next move will be to retire from the military and go prepare to campaign for a congressional run. My friend, I think you should do so too. Our country will need men who think like you, who have accomplished so much with so many obstacles in the way and barriers to break through. Stick to this path and you will should see only success. Ma'am, I'd like to thank you on behalf of my company and I know my mother would thank you as well. Take care and god bless," and after shaking hands, he bowed and passed through the front gates with his company of men following.

After the last man walked away, the family breathed a deep sigh of relief, and Regina spoke first saying, "Well, I can finally let out the breath I've been holding since they arrived. Who knew we'd meet such a well mannered and accomplished young northerner, shelter him from harm and send him home to his mama, without so much as a wrinkle between his men and ours. I think I wore the caps off my knees I've been on the floor so long. How are all of you feeling?" she asked turning to the rest.

"Mama, I'm glad we were able to help them, but I'm with you. I can breathe easier and sleep well tonight. It's almost over. Big Mama how are you feeling?"

"Glad they're gone, but I felt a sense of protection while they were here. Our men are ready for anything, but knowing that the Colonel and his men had our backs brought me comfort. Are you relieved or sadden Joseph?" she asked her new husband, moving closer into his arms.

"Bout the same as you I guess. We have worked so hard to ready ourselves that had he brought a different face forward, we would have had to deal with that. I'm glad for him that he was able to walk away unharmed, and like he said, glad for his mother too. However he chose to present himself, we were ready to accommodate him. His life was in his hands, right Henry?"

"Right. I know it's a little early, but this successful conclusion is an occasion. I say let's take the day to celebrate. I'll break out a bottle of that champagne in the cellar, and meet you all in the solarium in ten minutes."

Before he ran to the cellar, he got on his horse and rode down to his cottage to get Tawnie. He also wanted her to be in on the celebration. He quickened his pace after remembering their conversation not long ago. He jumped down from his horse and hurried inside. She was there, sitting in his gift to her, a lovely rocking chair crafted by one of the men as a gift to Henry's family in appreciation for what they had resolved in their hearts to do in changing history for the people. She looked lovely, with her hair pinned up, a soft bundle of yarn on her lap and knitting needles in her hands. He went to her and got down on his knees in front of the chair and she sat the project aside and took his head between her hands, saying, "Henry, I know what you were thinking, and you've got to stop. You'll make yourself miserable if you continue to worry about it. Try and enjoy the moment, and don't worry about the next hour. If not you'll miss what's in front of you, reaching for what's next. Now, what did you come rushing in here for?"

"We're going to celebrate the Colonel and his men's successful departure. Come dear one, come with me up to the house. I need you by my side. Have I told you how lovely you look today?"

"Yes, before you left, but a woman can never have enough praise, you know. Thank you my heart, you look wonderful also."

They rode together back to the main house and into the solarium. Regina noticed that Henry was much calmer than he'd been earlier and she knew it was because he had Tawnie by his side. She saw the love he had for this young woman who seemingly appeared from nowhere, and wondered when Henry would ask her to marry. She was surprised what she did hear when Henry held his glass up and announced, "Everyone, I am soon to be a father. Tawnie is carrying my child. Congratulations mother, you are to become a grandmother. Are you ready for that?"

Everyone gasped and smiled, offered congratulations and toasted to the health of the next generation. Regina fought the tears for a moment, then let them come. "Son, I wondered when I would get a daughter-in-law and some grandbabies. Thank you and welcome to the family Tawnie. To you both," and raised her glass. Everyone raised their glasses and drank another toast. Henry and Tawnie just smiled at each other, realizing the sadness it would bring to say that there would be no marriage. They weren't prepared for Regina's next question, but adlibbed when she said, "So when is the wedding? Are you going to try and do a rush job because of the baby or wait until after the birth?"

Henry looked at Tawnie and Tawnie spoke up first saying, "Well, we've talked about both ways but are thinking along the lines of waiting until after the birth, taking a trip to Paris for our wedding and honeymoon after the war. We're sure it will be over in a few months."

"So I'm understanding you to say the family won't be at the wedding?"

"Mother, let's all wait and see after the baby is born. I don't want Tawnie stressed about any plans other than delivering a healthy son or daughter for now. She's been through more than you can imagine. We might take you all and sail to France after the delivery, we don't know yet. Is that okay with you all?"

"Whatever you say son?" Regina stated somberly.

"I'm so glad for you both. I knew good things would happen when I first met you honeychile," Flora told Tawnie, winking her eye.

"Congratulations to you both. Flora and I would love to take you up on that trip to France," Joseph said, smiling.

21 CHAPTER

While everyone waited for the birth of Henry's firstborn, Henry and Tawnie spent practically every hour together. She knit, crocheted and stitched lots of lovely baby clothing and blankets for the upcoming bundle of joy. The women would often join her, drinking tea, sitting around working on their own pieces, being amazed at the designs she crafted, not knowing they weren't her original designs but were found in every shopping center in 1983. Or whatever year it was back home. The women copied the designs and began filling the store shelves with the pieces. Tawnie looked forward to each new day, enjoying her pregnancy. She was doted on by everyone. This was in her eyes just another baby, but not to those who'd lived and worked here, who'd cared for and known Henry his entire life. Even Marcus sat up and took notice. He was clean and sober for now, and the rest of the family tried not to drink in his presence, but Regina told them that no one should change their way of enjoying themselves because he could no longer handle his liquor.

Then the day came in the spring of 1865 when Marcus read that the southern confederacy had surrendered. He read in the newspaper dated two days before that Lee's army fought a series of battles that ultimately took his numbers of men to such a level that he could no longer offer a defense. Grant took advantage of the depletion and fought gallantly, which led to the surrender of Lee and the Army of Northern Virginia at Appomattox. Marcus read that, stood up to speak to Regina, and fell dead of a massive heart attack.

He was laid out in the front room and a notice was put in the papers. The burial was set to take place on the land, and that Sunday all his friends from surrounding plantations and towns attended. No one celebrated the way they usually did for one of their own because they were too disheartened hearing of Lee's surrender. They knew that it was just a matter of time before all the different regiments surrendered. They were right, and by November of 1965 they all had.

Whatever happened next was missed because the birth of Henry's son, Henry Robert Hazelton Jr. upstaged everything. Tawnie labored for only four hours before Nora, assisting at her side, encouraged her to push their son into Henry's waiting hands. Nora showed him how to cut the cord, clean away the mucus, slap his butt and wrap him before placing him into Tawnie's waiting arms. Too say he was pleased was too insignificant of a word for what Henry felt. He was over the moon with joy and excitement. As the baby nursed from her breasts, Henry was entranced, watching every detail. Tawnie told Flora, if he could he would want to nurse the baby from himself, that's how close he stayed under Tawnie.

As the weeks flowed into 1866, wherever the baby went Henry was soon to follow. The two could not be separated. One of the women made Henry a blanket sling that wrapped around his body so that he could take the baby with him around the land. The plans Henry made drove everyone crazy. He bought Robbie, his son's nickname they finally decided on, everything in sight including a brand new foal from his favorite mare. At just six months of age Henry began placing Robbie in the new body sling and riding around the land with him hanging from his own body.

Tawnie knew that when the time came, if it came, Robbie would be left here with his father. No way could she ever see a way of separating the two, nor would she want to. She had given birth to two sons already, and knew a father's love. Henry would die of a broken heart within six months she knew, if he had to be away from his child. Women were sometimes able to cope better when dealing in matters of the heart, than even the strongest man. And in this instance she knew that if she were transported back, she would leave Robbie and be able to live with her decision.

The water was open to all traffic now, and a trip was planned. This trip was to be only to the Caribbean for now. Henry wanted to take Flora and Joseph to see the new baby born to one of Marcus and Flora's sons. And of course he wanted to show off Robbie to his half-brothers too. While plans were being made, Tawnie gathered Robbie's diapers and all the things he would need, went to Henry and asked him if it would be okay to take Shayla and her children along. Over the last few months, Tawnie had spent a lot of time with Robbie visiting Shayla and her children for a purpose. She wanted to make sure her choice for Henry was also willing, able, and wanted to care for her baby if she returned to her other life. Shayla proved herself capable of being willing to care for Robbie, so Tawnie sat her down for a talk saying, "Shayla, I want to ask you if it's possible that you could love my baby and take care of him if anything happened to me? Yes his father would be there for him, but I would want him to also know the love of a woman, the love of siblings and the care from someone who knew me and what I hold dear. If you said yes, I would write up a official document that leaves you as his co-guardian along with Henry. Then if something were happen to Henry, Robbie would be placed souly in your care and no other relative, which would happen if I did not leave the document. I would ask Henry to leave a similar document too. They would be with his attorney and you would keep a copy also."

"Tawnie, I have honestly come to love you like a sister, and Robbie like my nephew. If anything happens to you I would gladly accept him as my own son. I plan on staying here as long as I am wanted, and given time may seek out my own man. Right now I'm trying to get my babies raised to an age that they feel comfortable staying with a teacher and other children for a few hours a day. By the way, I love the program for children that you encouraged the new teachers to begin. Aren't they wonderful?"

"Yes, I think so too. Thank you so much for agreeing to take care of my baby. While you watch him, I better take a few minutes to write out the document. Being on the ocean anything could happen, so I would feel better if I know I'm prepared. I'll be here in the office, call if you need me."

"Okay. We'll be fine," Shayla told her.

After Tawnie completed the paternity documents, she asked for a carriage to be brought around. She wanted to make sure they were taken to the attorney before she got on the ship. Not thinking about anything happening to the ship or the people, but about her own situation. She drove into town by herself, and left letters to Henry expressing her gratefulness and love to him and the family. She also asked the attorney to keep several of the pearls from the necklace for Robbie, giving the attorney a letter for him to read when he turned eighteen. When she felt that all was in order, she headed back to Hazeltown. With the pearl necklace tied up in a scarf inside her cloth purse, she began to feel light headed, and started to tremble. While trying to control the horses, but swaying from side to side because of dizziness, the carriage tumbled into a ravine and Tawnie went flying out of the carriage. She screamed and tumbled head over heels, landing on a soft mattress. When she got herself under control and sat up, she was back in her bedroom in the same plantation house that she shared with Bryen. She was home.

Sad but still relieved that she had made it back safely, she began crying and calling for Bryen and the children, "Bryen, I'm home. Ari, Miguel, Diego, mama's home. Where are you?" No one was home. Bryen was probably at work, and the children might be around somewhere with the Maggs their nanny or Jed and Rose. Tawnie decided to take a long hot bubble bath. The ones in 1800 could not beat those in 1983. She turned on the stereo and put on Rick James and Tina Marie singing Fire and Desire. While relaxing she thought about the way she left and wondered what her family back there would think happened to her. She was glad that Robbie had been left behind with Shayla when she went into town, because he might have been thrown and not traveled forward with her. What a relief that she hadn't wanted to take him. If there was another upside to this, that was going to be one that she was ever thankful for. Oh, my goodness, she thought, I'll have to go find the cemetery and see if the family is out there. That will have to wait; I don't think I can stand to see my loved ones names written down knowing I'll never see them again. I remember when I finally saw Granny's gravesite. It was more painful then hearing about her death and attending the funeral. My thoughts are so morose, I wish my family was here, she thought. The song wasn't soothing her just causing her to long for something she could never have again. Better to put all that happened behind her, and hope that her plans were carried out and that they all lived happy lives. She began to cry again.

Bryen found her asleep on their bed, had the shock of his life and eased his way into bed next to her. He just wanted to feel her next to him again. It had been six long months without her, and he was still trying to recover from her absence, even though he knew she would return at some point. He thought the necklace would help her return if she kept it nearby, and wanted to return to him. He curled up against her back and waited for her to wake, but instead fell asleep himself. When she woke up with a body resting against her, she turned around and found Bryen. She said, "Bryen, sweetie wake up. Oh, baby, I'm finally back. How are you and the kids?"

"Hello my love. I knew you'd return to me. We're all good, just missed you. It's been six months and I've had to put the kids off with excuse after excuse. Never put that necklace on again, okay?"

"Never. Guess what? It was two years over there. I was here but during the Civil War. Oh baby, it was crazy. But, with what I knew, I think I made a difference not only for the Hazelton's but for many others as well. So only six months passed here? That's not as bad as two years, huh?"

"No, not as bad, but pretty bad. Oh, how we missed you. How do families do it without two parents? And we have a lot of help, but the kids kept crying for you, running around here looking for you. I just kept saying look for her, she's probably here somewhere. Then I'd say, she might have gone to see her own mommy and daddy, and all the sisters. It was crazy!"

"How's Maggs, Rose and Jed?"

"They are all fine. I had to tell them of course, and they've been worried, but we all pulled together for the children. Good thing you didn't arrange to have any book club meetings yet, because with everything I put your family in Illinois through, mercy! I don't know how your parents did it, accepting what I told them, but they did. I was sure they would be down here, thinking I had done something to you."

"I bet," Tawnie added. "Well, it's over now. I'll let you handle the necklace from here on out."

"What? It might take me off somewhere. What if I had to do the Civil War all over again, and maybe as a soldier! No thanks."

"Hahaha! You're so crazy. Where are my babies now?"

"Maggs took them to the zoo, or at least that was the plan this morning when I left for work. I really couldn't say. Did you look for a note?"

"Not yet. I was so dizzy. I was in a buggy by myself returning from town, and got thrown, landing here on the bed. I was so scared, but relieved I landed on a soft spot instead of where I was headed, in a ditch."

"Well that's a blessing. Two years huh? How'd you endure it?"

"It was hard, but I kept telling myself 'I'm here for a reason.' I kept busy too since there was a lot to do, preparing the families that were enslaved to get ready for freedom. I even helped fight in a couple skirmishes against the southern rebels. That was scary, but with a little modern ingenuity and old-world skills, we worked it out and beat them."

"So you were here all the time, just not quite here. Who was the owners, or has the land always been in the Hazelton family?"

"As far as I know it has been. All the families even after the emancipation agreed to keeping the name so that they could trace their relatives to here, and any that had been sold before Henry, Regina, Marcus and Flora's children took over as custodians of the land. What we need to do in a few days is go and look for the cemetery that should be beyond that little cottage that we thought was a place for overflow relatives visits. The one we haven't even explored yet. There will be so much to look for now that I know where to look. Oh! Right now let's go up in the attic. I was told there would be many more treasures from the stuff the family used. The white family in the big house."

"Are you sure you're ready for that? I don't want you doing too much?"

"Bry, I've been on this bed the whole day, except for my bubble bath which was as good as I remembered. That's one thing, besides Colgate toothpaste that I couldn't get exactly how I like; brushing my teeth and bathing. If we go look now, when the kids get back I can spend the time with them."

"Alright. Let's go. What's supposed to be up there?"

"The silverware, silver teapot and all the matching pieces. And, a surprise. Here, can you pull that handle. It looks like the stairs are the pull down kind. Good."

"Now you have me excited. Some of your family treasures, wow. Did they say what you're supposed to do with them?"

"Yes. Find the family, set up a foundation, help everyone out with moving past any negative circumstances and organize an annual family reunion, using this house as the base."

"Really? They gave you all those details huh? Do you know any other names except Hazelton?"

"No, but I think once we have a look at the records more may come from them. Now, I'm looking for a rolled up tube, or canvas. It's about four feet tall and three feet wide. And crates or chest that should be hidden, at least not right out in the open just in case looters got in."

"Okay. Let's split up. I'll take the left half and you the right. Call me if you find something heavy, and I'll come lift it."

"Of course. This is so exciting; I've always loved treasure hunts. There's going to be a need to have a lot of them because so many people probably left so many things hidden around the place. Some might have put them away and forgot about them. You know what we could use, Bry . . ."

"Tawnie! Come here. I think I found the tube."

"Oh? That was quick. Yes, that might be it. I'm sure there's probably more than one of these around here. Wait until you see this."

Tawnie was looking for her painting. She hoped Bryen couldn't tell that she had been carrying Robbie at the time. She doubted it, because then she hadn't even known. She would probably have to one day tell him about her son, but not right now; the loss was too new. She unrolled the tube and yes, it was her. Bryen gasped, and his mouth dropped open in what she thought was awe.

"Wow! Is this you or a relative?"

"It's me. Guess who painted it? A soldier from the Union army. Yes, we had a regiment of them camp out on the front lawn. Their Colonel was shot and had to be n
ursed. On their last day with us, he painted my picture and said he would return to help the people, teaching and painting more of the families portraits. How do I look to you?"

"You look beautiful. He captured more of you than I have ever noticed; your essence, depth, he captured you as mother earth, one who lives to give life to others. Stunning!"

"Thank you baby. I'm so glad you like it. We all thought he did a good job. Should we move it to the bedroom?"

"No, let's put it up above the couch in the living room, for all to see. I'm proud of you."

"Well, I'd like to keep looking around. Do you mind if I stay up here awhile, and please come get me when the kids get back?"

"Sure," he told her with a resounding kiss. "I've missed doing that Tawnie, and I am so relieved you're back."

"Me too. See ya in a bit."

22 CHAPTER

Tawnie took a couple of deep breaths and looked back at her picture. She was sad all of a sudden, sad because again, she was keeping secrets from the love of her life. The man who was always thinking about her and how to keep her from falling into morose. It wasn't that she was diagnosed as a depressive, just that she took negative events in, and relived them over and over, not being able to let things go without encouragement. Bryen was always her strength when she had none. Bryen deserved to know all, and she would give him that when she comfortable about doing so. For now, Robbie would stay hers alone.

She rambled around in the attic searching through crates for the things that Henry told her of. She finally found the silver in separate areas, remembering that Henry suspected that at some point there might be dishonest people living there or going through their possessions. This set she'd take down and use it at her book club meetings. Some of the others she clean up and share with family members that she planned on finding. Now she looked for the letters Henry promised he write. It took another hour of hunting before she found a hand carved letter box with her initials carved on the top. T. H. from E. S. all my love was burned in italic letters. She felt a catch in her heart beat, and choking in her throat. She opened the lid and pulled the dated letters.

1865, September

My darling girl, when you did not return after visiting the attorney I sent out a hunting party. All we found were the horses eating at the side of the road and the overturned carriage. I pray that you have returned home, and not anything worse. Though I'm sure if that were the case we would have found some sign. There was no sign, no blood, no part of torn clothing, so I'm sure you are home safe. Our little son is fine, and is calling Shayla mama. I know you wanted me to eventually marry her, so after two years we were untied in marriage. The trip you and I were planning, to take Big Mama and Joseph to the Caribbean went off smoothly. After that I took Shayla to the Bahamas instead of where I wanted to take you, Paris. I will write more at other times. For now know that you will always have my heart.

Yours, Henry

Tawnie cried, but in joy more than for her losses. She knew that they'd had a good life together because she saw the type of people they were, and she'd chosen Shayla.

Later that night after the children had returned, excitement shared, baths and storybook read, Bryen pulled out a bottle of champagne he'd found in a basement storage room next to the apartment of Rose and Jed. Tawnie knew exactly who had put it there.

"Look what I found love. Guess how much there is down there? Sixteen cases of twelve bottles each. When you find your relatives, bring them here for your first annual reunion, you'll have to toast to the Ol' Massa and his family. And when you give me our next son, we will name him after the man who loved you and cared for you so well."

Tawnie couldn't speak, she just stared at Bryen wondering how he knew that she had been loved as much as he loved her. She went to him and took him in her arms, kissing him deeply. She said quietly, "You remember that Stevie Wonder song, I was Made to Love Her?, the words go something like this, *Papa disapproved it, my mama boo hooed it, but I told them time and time again, that I was made to love her*

Well, that's our theme song, because I do know that you were made to love me, and I was made to *be* loved by you. So you keep saying and knowing that '*my baby loves me, worships and adores me*' because that is exactly how I feel about you my love. I will play that now on the piano and you sing to me, okay?"

"Okay, Tawnie."

EPILOGUE

"Tawnie, little Henry is crying. I suspect that he's wet and ready to nurse. Are you ready to rise and shine my beauty?"

"Yes, sweetheart. The party last night lasted longer than I thought it would. I guess everyone was having so much fun getting to know one another. Daddy and mama sure had fun, and so did all the girls. I'm so glad your family came with them. It was sure good to see everyone. The family will be expecting all of us for breakfast soon so I have to get up. Let me wash my face and I'll be right there."

"Okay, baby. I'll strip him out of his clothes and let him kick around on the diaper changing pad. Good morning baby, and smooches."

"Back at ya."

It took eighteen months to locate every one of the Hazelton's and to put together the first annual Hazelton Clan Family Reunion. Little Henry was born ten months after Tawnie's return. Altogether, Henry wrote her thousands of letters; just enough in each one to let her know that he did indeed have a wonderful life, surrounded by his children and grand-children. Tawnie's father was descended from his side of the family, whether from the white side or the black side no one knew or cared. At the reunion, there were people of all colors under the sun and that's what mattered to them the most. Everyone had what they needed as far as what money could buy, for the rest of their lives. Each celebration included a toast to the forefathers who paved the way for their futures.

The End

ACKNOWLEDGEMENTS

Thank you so much for taking the time out to buy, read, and leave a review of my latest book.

This book was written not to encourage the belief in anything other than that we can make Agape`, principled love work, as long as we are willing to put in the time and effort it takes to give of ourselves to someone else. Isn't that what life is about?

This book is dedicated, of course to those asleep in death, but most of all to the living, to my daughter Brie and my husband Richard. Also to the friends who let me borrow a few things from them, and they know who they are. Thanks. Toni M. (☺)

ABOUT THE AUTHOR

Thanks for your purchase, and taking the time to read what I wrote and know that I appreciate your choosing me out of the million choices you could have made. I live in Wisconsin now, but was raised in Illinois. My great-great grandmother was from a nation in Africa, but the man who took her and created my grandmother was Scots-Irish. Her name was Robertha, and her mother the African was Rebecca. My aunt, my mother's sister found the white siblings of my great grandmother and relatives from that side of the family and they are now communicating. Life in this world is hard for all men, so instead of beating our heads against brick, we roll with life and do what we can to make it better. Those who look beyond their own circumstances are happier. Toni.

CPSIA information can be obtained
at www.ICGtesting.com
Printed in the USA
LVOW10s2027030517
533142LV00015B/279/P